COLLECTING SECRETS

PE KAVANAGH

BOLD
SOUL
BOOKS

COLLECTING SECRETS

For information contact : Pascale Kavanagh

http://www.pekavanagh.com

Cover designed by Olivia Pro Designs and Bliss Designs

E-book ISBN: 978-0-9994679-4-7

Paperback ISBN: 978-0-9994679-5-4

First Edition: February 2018

10 9 8 7 6 5 4 3 2 1

For Bear,
whose relentless dedication to research
ensured that I get a particular type of scene
just right.

CHAPTER 1

*T*his was not the first time Camille had looked foolish, but it might have been the first time she didn't care. Unable to find her room key or hold back the torrent of tears, she plunked down onto the ugly hotel carpet in front of her door and sobbed, loud and hard. With nothing but the back of her hand to wipe away the tears and snot, the scene quickly escalated from tragic to gruesome.

Heartbreak was no stranger. But this break-up was beyond humiliating. How dare he? She had given him everything and he claimed it wasn't enough. He'd stood in the cold marble lobby and yelled at her. Accused her of cheating. In front of everyone.

Humiliation mingled with anger and desperation, halting any effort to pull herself together. They'd flown across the country to attend this wedding and now she'd be conspicuously dateless in a room full of happy couples. She tried to take a breath and choked on a new wave of tears.

A soft crush of footsteps stopped in front of her, but Camille had no interest in lifting her head off her knees to look.

"Hey, Cam. What's wrong?"

She knew that voice, as well as the gentle stroke of his hand in her hair.

"Camille. You're scaring me. What's going on?"

His worry pierced through her pain and, with great effort, she tilted her head up to see her best friend's face inches from hers.

His eyes flashed to fear. "Camille! What happened? Are you okay? Talk to me!"

It took so much energy to form words. "Calm down, Jack. I'm okay."

"You don't look okay. Did something happen with Charlie? Where is he?"

The questions were coming too fast for Camille's throbbing, blurry head. "He dumped me." There, she said it. Out loud.

The line of his lips flattened and his breath growled. Rage filled his expression. "That mother fu-"

Camille shook her head, trying to regain her composure. "We flew all the way here and that bastard couldn't even wait one more day."

Jackson's mouth softened. "I'm so sorry." He rubbed his thumb across her cheek.

She looked into the warm brown eyes of her closest friend, the man who'd been like a brother for the past ten years. This was how she knew him best – kind, caring, and sweet. She didn't care how the world saw him. She had gotten to know the real man.

"Let's get you up and into your room." He slipped his long arms under hers and stood her up. She fell into his broad chest, melting into the arms that enveloped her.

"Where's your key, love?" he whispered into the top of her head.

She mumbled into his chest. "I couldn't find it."

Keeping a firm grip around her with one arm, Jackson dipped down to pick her purse up off the ground. "Can I take a look?"

"Of course." She had no secrets from him.

She winced when he had to unlock his arm from her waist to search through her purse. Of course, he knew exactly where she would have put the key: in the smallest zippered pocket.

He waved it in front of the magnetic pad and the loud click confirmed his success.

As expected, the room had been cleared of all Charlie's belongings. His compulsiveness would have prevented him from forgetting anything. Camille stepped away from Jackson to look around, hoping to find a belt, or a tie, or even a tube of shaving cream. Any excuse to contact him again. But there was nothing, not even a stray hair.

Charlie had almost snuck out without her knowing. If she hadn't had to leave the restaurant to go to the bathroom, she would never have seen him, bags in hand, striding across the lobby.

Jackson stepped in front of her, halting her examination of the room, and began wiping her eyes and nose with a tissue.

"I'm a mess." Only the slightest tinge of self-consciousness colored the moment. This was who they were and had always been. He pressed the tissue across her nose and she blew, like a small child.

"No, Cam. You're just hurting." He balled up the tissue and flicked it into the small metal bin to his right. "I know you're upset, love. But, personally, I'm glad he's gone. He was never good enough for you. And he reinforced his complete lack of class by doing this here. I mean, he couldn't have ended it before flying to Chicago with you?"

Camille dropped her head, another rush of tears pressing against her eyes.

His broad palms cupped her face, tilting her up to look at him. "Hey, hey, Cam. He has no idea what an amazing woman you are. There are better things in your future. I know it."

His shoulders lifted as he took a deep breath. Something about the look on his face locked her attention on him. When he touched his lips to hers, a first in their relationship, a tiny spark of surprise jolted her awake. When he pressed in, more deeply, passionately and deliberately, gripping her and parting her lips, there was no question a line had been crossed.

A column of heat filled Camille's body as his mouth explored hers. She could not have imagined anything as wonderful as that kiss in that moment. Until she remembered to whom that mouth belonged.

She pushed him away and covered her mouth with the back of her hand. Tears rolled down her cheeks. "Jack... what are you doing?"

He looked like a cornered animal, eyes darting, chest pulsing with quick, shallow breaths, expression frozen. "Cam..."

Her body began to shake. "Why did you do that?!"

"I... because... I..." He took two steps back and bumped into the desk behind him. "I'm sorry. I shouldn't have..."

Camille dropped her hand away from her face and stared at her closest friend. Her lips tingled. She did not like the feelings consuming her body. He was not hers to have in this way.

Jackson pressed his lips together briefly before speaking. "I messed up. My timing sucks. I'm sorry." He stepped toward the door. "I'm gonna go now, okay? I'll see you at the rehearsal dinner. I'm sorry about what happened today."

After the heavy door clicked shut, Camille stripped off her clothes, released the tight bedding, and laid her body down. It didn't matter that it was the middle of the day.

She closed her eyes, avoiding the most obvious question and instead lingering on the least traumatic. *What had he meant about his timing?*

～

CAMILLE THREW off the blankets and grumbled. The last thing she wanted to do was get all dressed up and make nice with the large party assembled for the rehearsal dinner. As a bridesmaid, however, she had no choice but to attend. It had been a grueling day and not even burying herself under the covers for a couple of hours had brought relief from the double whammy. First, the tactless breakup, and then a surprise kiss from the one man from whom she would have never expected such a thing.

She hadn't thought of Jackson that way since their earliest days, back when she had just entered Princeton. Of course, she'd had a crush on him. He had that effect on every woman he met. But when they built a relationship based on trust, respect, and friendship instead of sex, it felt exactly right.

He was a playboy, never without a glamorous woman on his arm, but her position as his closest friend was much more important and stable. She had no interest in being part of the temporary arm candy parade. But the kiss that lingered on her lips refused to be ignored.

The enormous wedding party was already seated when she arrived. All that hemming and hawing made her late.

Emma, the bride-to-be, scurried to meet her. "Cam, I heard what happened. I'm so sorry sweetie. Are you okay?"

Camille didn't want her bad news to affect her friend's wedding celebrations. "I'm perfectly fine, Em. It was for the best. And we're here to celebrate you, anyway. Nothing sad today!"

Emma gave her a crooked smile. "Okay. But you let me know if you want to talk."

Camille forced a grateful smile. "Sure will."

She scanned the length of the immense rectangular table for her seat. It should have been easy to find: two empty seats next to each other. But the only opening was next to Jackson. He stood up abruptly as she approached the table. His chivalry did not make up for the fact he had clearly altered the seating arrangements.

He pulled out her chair and slid her into place. "You look beautiful, Cam. As always."

She couldn't look at him. Why wasn't he keeping his distance after their awkward moment? And where was his date? She could have sworn she was supposed to have arrived that afternoon. "Where's Anya?"

"She's not coming."

Camille spun around to glare at him. "What?!"

"I asked her not to come. She's shooting in Europe next week and I told her she'd probably be bored hanging out with all these people she doesn't know. It was never that serious, as you know."

Rage burned in her chest as she hissed out her response. "Are you kidding me? You disinvited her the day she was supposed to get here? You're no better than Charlie. Why would you do that?"

"I did it for you, Camille."

Jackson's calm deliberateness stood in stark contrast to the ruckus in Camille's body. If it wouldn't have caused a scene, she would have pushed away from the table, marched to her room, and spent the rest of the evening under her covers. She could not understand what had happened to the world around her.

Each course of the dinner, as delicious as it was beautiful, including a wonderful French plum tart, did nothing to counter the bitterness coating Camille's tongue. She had successfully kept her eyes straight ahead and her attention anywhere but to her left. As soon as they were excused to the lounge for after-dinner drinks, Camille made sure to put as much space as possible between herself and Jackson. But everywhere she looked, he was there, watching, with a look in his eyes that screamed nothing she wanted to hear.

She was swirling the olive in an untouched martini when her best friend Jenna found her. "Jack told me what happened today."

She couldn't believe he had told his sister about the kiss.

"I'm sorry Charlie hurt you, but I'm glad he's gone. He was a Grade A asshole. Good riddance, I say. So let's drink to that!"

"Jack told you about Charlie? Did he say anything else?" Camille took an overly large sip of her drink as she tried not to panic.

"Not really, no. Was there something else?"

Camille didn't want to lie to her friend, but this was not the time to get into it. "No, Jenna. Just that."

"We're all here for you, Cammy. You know that. And your date will now be the most handsome guy in the room."

Camille shivered. "What?"

"Jack. He'll be your date now. And nobody loves you more than he does."

Camille willed her face to stay calm. "Jenna-"

"I'm a close second, I know. Go have fun with my brother and forget all about that loser, Charlie."

Camille clinked the glass Jenna held up, then wiped out the remainder of her martini.

CHAPTER 2

TEN YEARS EARLIER

*C*amille dragged her enormous suitcase down the long hallway of her freshman dorm. This was the first day of her new life, far from home, officially on her own. Princeton University was where the new, better Camille would be created.

She tripped into her room, too busy checking the numbers on the doors to notice the gap in the old wood floors. A shockingly pretty girl sat on one of the small beds and looked up from her phone, startled.

"Hey!" Her smile lit up the room. "I'm Jenna. I guess we're roommates."

The first thought through Camille's mind was how could she be so unlucky to have the most beautiful girl in school as her roommate. The second thought was that it would be impossible to hate her.

"My name's Camille." She put out her hand. "Nice to meet you."

Jenna popped up, took Camille's arms, and pulled her away from the doorway. "Watch out!"

Two men, hidden behind stacks of boxes, stumbled into the room.

"Guys! You almost ran over my new roommate! Could you be more careful?"

When the men put their boxes down, the offenders came into full view. The first one nearly knocked the breath from Camille's body. Certainly the hottest guy she had ever seen in person. Like a sexy gladiator after a fashion makeover who'd been transported through time to her dorm room.

"Jen, you must be kidding. We're slaving away, carrying all your shit while you sit there on the phone, and you're yelling at us?"

Jenna went over to him and wrapped her arms around his waist. "Sorry, Jack. You're the best. I mean it."

The other one cleared his throat.

"You too, Justin." She stood between them and put one arm around each. "Camille, these are my favorite people in the whole world. My big brother Jackson, and my baby brother Justin. Guys, this is my roommate and soon-to-be best friend in the world."

Camille forced herself to stop staring at Jackson's square jaw, perfect ebony hair, and bright white smile. She had to pull it together. "Hi guys. Nice to meet you. Most people call me Cammy."

Jackson shook her hand. "Cammy it is, then."

So entranced by his large hand and broad shoulders, she nearly missed the small wave from Justin. The guys headed out of the room, grumbling about all the boxes.

As if nothing had happened, Jenna turned her attention back to Camille. "Where are you from, Cammy?"

"San Francisco."

"Holy shit! Me too! I didn't think there were that many west-coasters here. What are the chances?"

Camille nodded. "And your brothers came all the way across the country to help you move? That's amazing."

"Actually Jackson lives in New York. He's a grad student at Columbia. A real smarty pants. And I think my parents bribed Justin to come out. My other brother Julian was too busy with school, but I'm sure you'll meet him eventually too."

An impression formed in Camille's head: Jackson, Julian, Justin and Jenna. This sounded more like a cult than a family.

"Is your family here too?"

Camille didn't want to bring out the tragic story just yet. "Ummm, they'll be here… later."

"Cool." Jenna returned to her phone.

When Jenna's parents strode into their room, the whole picture snapped into place. Her mother was an older, more elegant version of Jenna - tall, slender, meticulously dressed with a head of blonde hair in a shade you just couldn't buy. Her father had dark hair and eyes, just like Jackson, and was nearly as handsome. Camille wondered if they were the poster family for her Ivy League school.

"Hello, you must be Jenna's roommate." Her mother even sounded beautiful.

"Yes, ma'am. My name is Camille."

"Oooh, what a lovely name. Reminds me of romance, and Paris, and-"

Her husband interrupted. "Darling…"

"Right… I'm Elena, Jenna's mom, and this is Jonathan, her dad. I think you met the boys already?"

"Yes, I did. Nice to meet you all."

Jenna addressed her parents. "Cammy is from San Francisco too! Can you believe it?"

"Well, that's quite extraordinary. You two can pine for the Bay Area together."

"I'm not going to pine, Daddy. I'm going to love it here." Jenna turned to Camille. "My mother went here and met my Dad. So there might be big things ahead for us, Cammy!"

A giggle slipped out. Boys would be such a refreshing topic in Camille's life. "I hope so."

"Enough talk about boys, please. I'm already traumatized enough that my baby girl is so far away from home." Jonathan tucked his daughter under his arm and kissed the top of her head.

"Don't worry, Daddy. Grades before boys."

"You got it, sunshine."

A small crack in the middle of her chest forced Camille to brace herself. This was not the time to drown in sadness. This was a new start, a chance to move forward. She compelled herself to smile and appreciate the lovely family in front of her.

It took several trips to the car to retrieve the rest of her bags. She'd shipped most of her belongings, but they hadn't yet arrived. Good thing, because between Jenna's family and all of Jenna's stuff, there was hardly room for Camille.

She sat on the center of her bed, trying to be as inconspicuous as possible while stealing glances at Jackson. If college guys looked like that, Camille was going to have the time of her life. She had lots of catching up to do after her dreadfully chaste high school years.

Jenna hopped up onto the bed with her, breaking Camille's focus on Jackson's outstanding rear end. "Come to dinner with us, Cammy." Her new best friend beamed at her. "We're going out to celebrate and you can bring your family, and…"

"Actually, they won't be here today." Another white lie wasn't going to hurt.

"An even better reason for you to join us," Jackson chimed in.

Camille swallowed. "Sure. Okay. Thanks."

"Awesome!" Jenna gave her a hug.

Camille tried not to bristle. It was strange being enveloped by this large, affectionate family. So unfamiliar that it bordered on surreal. Even when her parents were still alive, it had just been the three of them, and they were never like this. She hugged Jenna back and decided that this was how her new life was going to look: beautiful and surrounded by love.

THE TWO YOUNG women sat on Camille's bed for hours, talking about boys and shoes, then ended up having to scramble to get ready for dinner. Camille emptied her suitcase onto the bed, trying to remember what she'd packed that would work for that night's outing. Everything on the East Coast was so much more formal than her laid back California home. Not to mention that she wanted to strike the right balance of pretty and elegant without looking too sexy.

She chose a simple navy shift. Camille's abundance of curves made most dresses that looked nice on other bodies take a turn for the pornographic on hers. Even though Jackson would be there, she decided it wasn't going to be the best night to put the full throttle of boobs and butt on display.

"Oh my God, is that the new Dolce?" Jenna was already dressed, hands on hips.

Camille smoothed down the front of the dress. "It's only last season."

"Well, it's gorgeous. I could never pull off a dress like that. I'd look like a little boy."

Camille scrunched her nose at the woman in front of her, who happened to be stunning. "No way, Jenna. I'm sure there's nothing you couldn't wear."

The knock on the door prevented the conversation from going any further.

Justin stepped into the room and gave his sister an exasperated look. "We're all waiting in the car. Come on!"

They arrived at the restaurant and followed single file as the hostess led them through the packed dining room. They were clearly not the only ones with the idea of a family dinner on move-in day. As they approached the large rectangular table, Camille willed herself to relax and enjoy what was happening around her: smiles, laughter, tenderness. She could get used to this.

She took the seat between Jenna and Elena, and watched as Jackson sat directly across from her. His tee shirt and scruffy jeans from that afternoon had been replaced by a shirt nearly the same color as her dress, and dark slacks. He'd shaved. She didn't know how she was going to stop herself from staring at him, as he was even more gorgeous than earlier that day. She glanced up to find him looking at her with such sweetness that she imagined falling in love with him, right there on the spot. Too bad it would have to stay a fantasy, as he was miles outside of her reach.

Elena gazed at her with a smile. "I've been having fantasies about Paris all day, Camille, inspired by your beautiful name. Tell me you have a French last name too, and I will dissolve."

"Yes, actually. It's Moreau."

"Oh, that's so familiar. I've definitely heard that name before." She turned to her husband. "Honey, don't we know somebody named Moreau?"

Her husband shook his head very slowly, perhaps already knowing where this was going.

"Yes, yes, I'm sure." Elena tapped her upper lip with an elegant fingertip. "Wait! There was a San Francisco couple who died not long ago. Plane crash, I think. He was a prominent judge. Are you related to them?"

Even before Camille answered, a look of horror washed over the other people at the table. Perhaps it was because of the pain that filled her expression. Perhaps it was the boom of her heart. "Yes, ma'am. Those were my parents."

Elena gasped. "Oh my God, Camille!" Her voice trembled with panic. "I am so sorry. I had no idea. How thoughtless of me. If I had known, I would have never-"

"It's okay, Mrs. King." Camille kept her eyes focused on the items directly below her gaze. A plate, a fork, two glasses...

Jenna touched the top of her shoulder. "I'm so sorry, Cammy." Her voice shook.

When she finally gathered the strength to look up, Camille took in the full view in front of her - a furrow in his brow, sadness in the molten chocolate eyes, and a slight part of his perfect lips. Compared to all the expressions of sympathy and pity she had received in her short life, this one, from a near stranger, penetrated the deepest.

IT WASN'T EVEN the end of freshman year and this was the third of Jackson's epic parties Camille and Jenna had been invited to. As they sat on the train into Manhattan, the girls tittered about all of Jackson's hunky friends. There was only one man Camille really cared about. She had it bad for her best friend's older brother. Maybe this would be the night she'd end up in his bed. Not that she would know what to do once she got there.

It didn't matter that he was way out of her league. He didn't treat her like the oddity she feared she was, but he didn't treat her like a woman, either. More like a little sister. She was willing to wait patiently for him to notice her in a different way. Jackson King was the catch of a lifetime.

Bodies flowed in and out of his massive Soho loft through the night. Even past the hour that Camille thought anyone would still be up and about. By three A.M. it had finally quieted down enough to consider trying to sleep. She was exhausted and every spare surface had been taken over by bodies in various states of drunkenness and sexual exploration. Jenna's romp with the DJ in the spare bedroom prevented Camille from taking her normal sleeping spot, so she ended up at Jackson's door.

She tapped on the doorframe.

Jackson rolled over on the bed to face her. The sheets fell to his abdomen. "What's up, fry?"

She forced herself to focus on the glass of water on the bedside table instead of that unbelievable male body barely covered by crisp white sheets. "Need somewhere to crash."

He patted the large space next to him. "Come on in."

She crossed her arms and stood in the doorway. "You'll have to put on a shirt first."

"Are you serious? It's fine. There's plenty of room in this bed."

Yes, there was room for at least three people in Jackson's enormous bed. That didn't matter. "Please put on a shirt."

He swung his legs around and pushed himself out of bed. Despite her best efforts, she could not turn away as he stomped over to the chest of drawers and pulled out a tee shirt. Camille would never tire of looking at the perfection of his body.

He pulled the shirt over his head, turned to face her, and lifted his arms out to the sides. "Better?"

She padded over to the opposite side of the bed, got in, pulled the covers up under her chin and answered. "Yes. Thanks."

She could hardly feel the dip as he lay down, but his presence so close to her wreaked havoc in her body. What was she thinking?

Out of the corner of her eye, she saw his back was turned to her.

"I can feel the tension in your body all the way over here, Cammy. Are you okay?"

"Yeah." Her voice cracked. "Just fine."

"You don't sound fine." He rolled over to face her, lingering on her eyes. "Cam, are you a virgin?"

It was inevitable that she and Jackson went deep and personal, fast. This had been the tenor of their relationship from day one. "Yeah. So what?"

"Don't get defensive there, fry. I'm not judging you. I'm just trying to figure out why you're so… uncomfortable."

Because I'm in bed with the hottest guy I know. Who I happen to be in love with. "What does one thing have to do with the other?"

"You know you're 100% safe here, with me, right? You have nothing to feel concerned about."

She crossed and uncrossed her ankles. "I've gotten pretty close a few times. I'm not a total newb."

"There nothing wrong with waiting. You're just a kid, still."

"First of all, I'm almost nineteen, just a few years younger than you. Second of all, having your parents crash into the side of a mountain halfway through high school tends to put a damper on the whole dating thing."

He swallowed and softened the molten chocolate of his eyes. "I'm so sorry, darlin'. I seriously can't imagine how you even made it through high school, much less kicking ass and getting into Princeton. You have absolutely nothing to feel bad or ashamed about."

Camille fought back the wave of emotion that pressed into the back of her throat. "When did you lose your virginity?"

He lifted the corner of his mouth. The one near the dimple. "Nice redirect there, fry."

She matched his grin. "I learned from the best. Now spill it."

"I was a junior, sixteen I guess. A senior girl basically seduced me. I was her plaything until she graduated."

She squeezed her brows together. "I can't tell if that was a good thing or a bad thing."

"It was awesome. There's a reason why the cultural trope of boys being initiated by older, more experienced women exists. It's a system that works. Boys need instruction."

"Did you get instruction?"

"It was a start. I'm still learning."

"What are you learning?" The words came out well before her good sense stopped her.

He lifted up onto his elbow and looked down at her. "For someone who wouldn't even get in this bed without me putting on a shirt, you're getting into some pretty risqué stuff, fry."

"I never claim to be consistent. I am curious, though. I want to know." This part - talking about it - was easy. All the other stuff - not so much.

He lay back down so they were both staring at the ceiling, on opposite sides of the bed. "Okay, then. I'm learning that each woman is different. That I can master some trick or maneuver, but it might fall totally flat on the next woman. Being a good sexual partner seems to be more about paying meticulous attention to the one you're with, rather than having skills."

She considered his response. "That makes sense."

"And I'm not making any claims about having figured it out."

"But that's the whole point of your studies, right? The psychology of love and sex and stuff. So I'm sure you will." *I'm pretty sure you already have.*

"I hope so. It's a pretty kick ass field, I have to admit."

She released her hold on the blankets just a tiny bit.

"How about you, Cam? Do you think about... sex? Is there someone you're thinking about sharing that with?"

At least four circuits blew in her brain. The situation she found herself in was beyond ridiculous.

"Well, yes. Maybe."

"Not that you asked, but here's some big brother advice for you. Don't be afraid to make him wait. Let him earn that immense gift. And please, please, please be safe."

"Jenna's got a lifetime supply of condoms in our room. I'm sure I can steal a few. And maybe she'll be the experienced woman to initiate me."

Jackson spun around so fast that the whole bed shook. She burst out laughing at the expression on his face. "No, dummy, I didn't mean it like that. I just meant she seems to have the whole sex thing figured out. I'm sure I can ask her anything."

It took him a minute to regain his bearings. "Cam?"

"Yes, Jackson."

Everything around his eyes softened. "I want you to know that you can always come to me. Okay?"

It was then that Camille realized that the large space between them in the bed was filled with nothing less than the most twisted irony.

CHAPTER 3

NOW

*C*amille let herself exhale fully only after the covers were pulled over her head. Thank goodness the rehearsal dinner was over. If she'd had to hold herself together for even one more second, her hair might have caught on fire. She took her first full breath in her bed, snuggled in tight, far away from Jackson King.

Burrowed underneath a tent of sheets had been a safe space since childhood. Whenever the fighting began at home, she encased herself in the protective shield of her bedding. Even as an adult, without the impetus of her parents' angry voices, it was where she went for emotional comfort.

Camille's eyes adjusted to the dark enough to see some of the city lights filtering through the covers. She liked Chicago. If not for the winter weather, she could see herself living there. If there was enough time tomorrow, before the festivities began, she'd go for a run around the lake. It was still a bit chilly out, but she could work up enough of a sweat to keep her warm.

The first set of knocks on the door was muffled by the layers of blankets. The second set was indisputable.

"Who is it?"

"It's me, Cam. Let me in."

Camille squeezed her eyes shut, willing Jackson to go away.

"Camille, I will go downstairs, get a key, and let myself in. You know I can do that. Now, please, let me in."

She threw the covers aside and stomped to the door. Jackson had the ability to convince anyone of anything. She could resist his manipulations and was just as certain the front desk attendant could not. It wasn't only his doctorate in psychology, it was the essence of his power.

He was still wearing his suit from dinner, but his tie was gone, and the top buttons of his shirt were open. She forced her eyes to move from the enticing slice of his chest visible underneath the crisp white shirt.

"What do you want, Jack? It's late."

He gripped the edge of the door and gently pushed it open far enough to step through. She moved out of the way, but he did not enter the room any farther. His gaze lingered on the cartoon characters on her faded t-shirt. She crossed her arms, self-conscious that he could probably see the outline of her breasts, and then shook her head that this had become an issue.

He stepped around her, walked toward the window and turned around. The room was dark enough that his features were shadowed. "We need to talk about what happened today. I can't stand you avoiding me. It's killing me."

She shifted from one foot to the other. "It's okay. It was a momentary lapse of reason. We can just forget about it, alright?"

"I can't forget about it." He leaned back against the window ledge.

This was not the answer she expected. "I'm too emotionally raw to deal with this, Jack." She sat down on the end of the bed, her attention drawn to the expanse of thigh visible below her shirt.

"I love you, Camille."

"I love you too, Jackson. You're my-"

"You misunderstand." He walked the few steps toward her and sat next to her on the bed. "I love you. I'm *in* love with you."

Every other sense drowned underneath the pounding and rushing in her ears. This couldn't be happening.

"I know my timing sucks. I'm sorry for that. But I'm glad it's finally out. I've been waiting for you for a long time." He lifted his hand, then lowered it back to his lap. The look in his eyes reminded her of the first night they had met, when he looked at her across the large dinner table. After she'd told the truth about her family.

"I don't understand why you're doing this. And why now."

"There's nothing in my life that scares me more than losing you. I'm taking a big risk, Cam. You could tell me to fuck off, or slap me, or worse. So, I'm not doing this because it's easy. I'm doing this because… it's time."

"Time for what?"

"Time for us." His hand slipped under her hair and wrapped around the back of her neck. It took the slightest pull to bring her face to his, followed by a warm breath, and the sensation of soft lips moving hers apart. There was no point avoiding the obvious - her body responded to him - and she did nothing to separate them.

When her hand slipped under his open collar to touch the chiseled chest she had seen so many times, and his palm pressed into the top of her thigh, she knew that there was only one direction this night could go.

Camille had very successfully rationalized that physical intimacy would never be a part of their relationship. And yet, there they were, hands and mouths roaming and scouring each other.

"Stop." Her single word pulled his mouth from the top of her breast.

"Cammy…"

"This is too much for me." She could not find a word that adequately captured the love, desire, and respect she felt for the man who had been a lifesaver. She also knew that she'd successfully avoided this exact event for many years. "I won't lie and say I'm not..."

His body straightened, and he pulled away from her. "I understand."

The absence of his body on hers left a painful sensation somewhere between cold and numbness. "We need to think this through. What we have deserves consideration."

He burrowed his gaze into her eyes. "I couldn't agree more."

There they sat - inches apart, his hand on her back, her hand on his chest - for minutes.

He broke the silence. "I'm staying here tonight."

Camille blinked rapidly. "No. You -"

"Cam, I'm staying here tonight. Too much has happened today for us to be apart."

She didn't want him to go.

"You don't have to worry about anything. We've spent many nights in the same room. In the same bed, even. You know you can trust me."

There was no one on the planet she trusted more than Jackson King. The only question was: could she trust herself?

He stood up and eased her back onto the bed, where he tucked her in the blankets, just the way she liked it. Standing in front of her, with the city lights creating geometric patterns across his suit, he began to shed each of his layers. His jacket, then his shirt, each button undone more mesmerizing than the one before. Then his belt, and his pants, leaving him in dark boxers that clung to his remarkable body.

This was not the first time Camille had seen him like this. But never before had his body been an offer to her.

She fisted the sheets that separated the two of them, desperately praying for the feeling of desire to pass.

He walked around the bed, outside of her view, and slid

under the covers. The next sensation was of the front of his body - warm, angular, needy - curled against the back of hers.

"Good night, Camille."

Instead of forcing the response that was stuck in her throat, she took his arm and wrapped it tightly around her.

SHE AWOKE to the sensation of a hand on her breast and a man pressing into her back. When the realization of who those parts belonged to cleared her sleepy mind, her body jolted. He responded by pulling her hips and bottom into him.

"Jackson. Wake up."

Her assumption that he was asleep was incorrect. He shifted himself on top of her in one swift move. Before she could say anything more, his mouth was on hers.

Between the weight of his body and the tenderness of his lips, Camille struggled to find a reason not to continue. His hand explored the tender flesh of her breasts while his mouth took her in. Her fingers slid under the band of his underwear, squeezing a handful of his muscular ass.

She caught her breath as he pulled away, only to gasp as he dispensed with both her t-shirt and underwear. Before bringing himself back down, he stared, unapologetically, at her naked body.

"You are even more stunning than I imagined, Camille." He dropped his head and licked one of her nipples before pulling it into his mouth. The sensation of his teeth grazing against her pulled a yelp from the base of her throat. When his hand slid between her legs, the shock of it shattered the last of her sleepy and desire-laden daze, and emerged like a primal growl.

He looked up at her without pausing the gentle movement of his fingers. There was no hiding how ready she was for him. When he brought his fingers from inside her to his lips, her body quivered with need. His underwear came off with a combination of their hands and legs, and soon he was pressing into her. He nuzzled into the crook of her neck, panting her name. She forced herself to open her eyes, assaulted by the ugly speckled tiles of the ceiling.

She slid her palms under his hip bones and urged him away. "This can't happen."

He pushed up onto his hands and knees, and then dropped his head onto her belly. She ran her fingers through his thick, dark hair, while they both caught their breath.

"I don't know what to say." His lips hovered over her skin.

"You want to fuck me."

He jerked his head up. "Do you think that's what this is?"

She crinkled the corners of her eyes. "That seems indisputable, don't you think?"

"That's not what's happening here."

"How can you say that? I mean, look at us."

He scanned her body.

She drew her arm across herself. "That's not what I meant."

"This has nothing to do with wanting to fuck you."

Camille's eyebrows shot upward.

"Okay, yes, I want to fuck you. But that's not the whole of it."

"I think we should get up now. We're not making good choices. You need to go."

He pressed onto his knees, stepped off the bed and stood before her. She had, for so many years, stopped herself from imagining his body. The reality was much, much better than the fantasy anyway.

"I want to be perfectly clear, Camille. I am in love with you. I want you, as you have now seen. I'm going to leave, because you've asked me to. But there is absolutely nothing that's happened in the past day that I wouldn't call a good choice." He picked up his clothes, got dressed, and left her room.

∾

EIGHT YEARS earlier

Camille and Jenna walked up the three flights of stairs to Jackson's loft, excited to celebrate the end of sophomore year. It had been a tough one. As they struggled to keep up with the brilliant minds around them, Jackson was making impressive strides as an expert in the psychology of attraction. By the time he completed his doctorate, he was going to be world famous. At least, Camille thought so.

They stepped into the enormous and impressively messy space. Jackson strolled out of his room wearing long shorts and nothing else.

"How are my favorite girls?" A grin filled the lower half of his face.

His sister scrunched her nose in distaste. "Put on a shirt, Tarzan. We're not here to fawn over your pecs."

He ignored her, instead giving Camille a hug. "Hey, Cammy. Thanks for coming in to town."

She let herself settle against his chest, palms on his back. His amazing chest and back, carved like an Italian sculpture. She steadied herself. "Of course, Jack. We have to celebrate."

He leaned back to look her in the face. "My girls are halfway through college. Imagine that."

"I thought we were celebrating your article," added Jenna, straightening his couch cushions.

"Yeah, that too."

Camille stepped out of his arms, giving her a better perspective to see him. "Vanity Fair is no pulp rag. You did well, Jack."

He held on to her hands and smiled. "You guys decide where you want to go?"

Jenna busied herself cleaning off the coffee table. "Let's do the Village. That place where they know you and won't give us a hard time about our IDs."

"You two need to hurry up and turn twenty-one before we all get in trouble."

Jenna rolled her eyes. "Whatever." She walked into the

kitchen and deposited an armful of glasses in the sink. "Got anything to eat?"

"Yeah, there should be some Chinese leftovers in there. Have whatever you want."

"You know I will. Come on, Cammy, let's have a snack."

"I'll go get ready, then," he said, disappearing into his bedroom. Camille stood completely still, but in her mind, she stepped across the apartment, followed him in, and closed the door.

THEY WERE all intoxicated by the time they entered the third bar, in search of some dancing. They weren't fans of the stadium-sized clubs that filled Manhattan, opting instead for the packed bar with a tiny dance-floor. It was nearly impossible to move in the crush of bodies, but Camille found it exhilarating anyway. She was lost in the beat, the heat, and movement of her body when someone grabbed her arm. Her eyes snapped open to see Jackson's worried expression.

"Hey, where's Jenna?" Panic creased the middle of his forehead.

"I don't know, Jack. Last I saw, she was over by the bar. Maybe she's in the bathroom?"

"Could you go look, please? I'll check by the bar."

"Sure." A shiver ran down her back.

Camille scanned the room for Jenna's long blonde hair, distinctive in the huge crowd. Pushing her way through to the bathroom, she looked up and down the line. Still no sign of her. She continued back down the long corridor past the men's room. Jenna had always been a bit wild. Maybe…

Camille noticed the flash of blonde even though it was mostly covered by a large, dark shape.

Her heart rate doubled. "Jenna, is that you?"

"Get the fuck out of here," someone snarled at her. The man

moved his head just enough for her to see the side of Jenna's face, pressed against the dirty wall. Her eyes were glazed.

"Get off her, asshole!" Camille strode directly to the large man.

"What? You wanna join us? Three's fine with me." His lips parted as his eyes raked over Camille's body.

"Just let her go, okay? I need her to come with me." Camille's chest burned with fright. There's no way she could take this guy. And Jenna didn't look like she would be any help at all. Had he drugged her?

"We're not done yet. So either do something useful or scram." He turned his head back to Jenna and burrowed his face in the side of her neck.

Camille harnessed all her strength and pushed his arm. He barely budged.

"You're really starting to piss me off, bitch." He backed away from Jenna, and her body drooped onto the floor.

With each step he took toward Camille, she took one step back. Her eyes darted to either side searching for a way past him, or something she could use as a weapon. All she saw was the obscene graffiti scrawled on the walls, and seething rage in front of her.

"Don't even think about touching that girl!" The recognizable low growl echoed off the walls closing in on her. Thank God he'd found them!

Jackson's arm wrapped around the front of her waist and pulled her back. His heart beat through his shirt into her back, his breath blazed on the back of her neck. He spun her around so she was behind him and ordered her to go.

Camille took a few steps back, then turned around just in time to see the two men heading for each other. This was not going to end well.

"What do you think you're going to do here, kid? Be a hero?" A crazed grimace contorted the dirtbag's features.

"I'm just going to get my sister and go. I'm not looking for trouble."

Camille couldn't see Jackson's face, but his pace was steady. Nothing in his body signaled apprehension.

"Well you found it." The large man took a lumbering swing at Jackson, who was significantly faster and ducked under him. By the time the man turned around Jackson had run to his sister and picked her up.

Camille spun toward the bar to get help. She returned with two bouncers to a drastically different scene. Jenna was back on the floor, Jackson's nose was bleeding, and the large man was doubled over.

"That's him! In the jacket! He attacked my friend."

The bouncers stood the man up and dragged him the opposite way down the corridor, away from the main part of the bar.

"Wait! Don't we want to wait for the police? Where are they taking him?"

"It's okay, Cam. I'm okay. We don't need the police."

Jackson and Camille swiveled in the direction of the unexpected voice, then ran over to Jenna.

He moved the hair away from her eyes. "What happened, Jenna?"

"We came back here to make out, and he got a little... intense."

"Did he...?" Jackson asked the question Camille was afraid to.

Jenna's body convulsed. "No. He didn't have a chance. Cammy got here just in time."

Jackson pulled his sister up with one arm, put the other around Camille's shoulders, and marched them both out of the bar.

Camille struggled to keep up with his long strides and brisk pace. No one said a word.

When they entered his apartment, the women went into the bathroom, where Camille wet a washcloth and Jenna splashed water onto her face. The women's eyes met in the mirror.

"I'll be out in a minute. Why don't you check on Jackson?" Jenna spoke so softly, Camille had to read her lips in the reflection.

"Sure, sweetie."

Camille found Jackson in the kitchen, putting ice into a plastic bag. "How are you doing, Jack?"

He lifted his fingertips to the gash in the middle of his nose. "I'm okay. It's not broken."

"Here. Let me…" Camille took the washcloth and gently cleaned away the blood that had dried around his nostrils, cheek and upper lip. He closed his eyes and placed a hand on her shoulder to steady himself.

She removed as much as she could, revealing the beginnings of the inevitable bruise. "As good as new."

"Thanks, Cammy. I appreciate that. How's Jenna?"

"She's cleaning up. Maybe in shock."

He nodded. "And you?"

"I'm okay. Better than you or Jenna, I think."

He lifted her chin toward him. "That was really brave of you to confront that guy."

"I don't think I've ever been more scared in my life. I'm surprised I didn't vomit. He had Jenna pushed up against the wall and I thought he was-"

"Stop talking about me." Jenna emerged from the bedroom wearing one of her brother's Columbia tee shirts, which draped over her like a knee-length dress.

"Hey, bunny. How are you?"

"I'm okay. You guys saved my ass tonight. Sorry about the drama." Jenna dropped her head and took a few ragged breaths.

Camille walked toward her, watching the tears drop from Jenna's cheeks onto the front of her shirt. Jackson moved to his sister, bent down and scooped her up like a small child. Their immense size difference had never been so obvious. Camille followed the two of them to the large sectional, where Jackson sat down with Jenna on his lap.

She tucked herself into him and cried as he stroked her hair and whispered, "You're okay, bunny. I'm here. You're safe."

Camille sat across from them and watched. Raised in a family that never expressed this degree of tenderness, she was mesmerized. It was at that moment she made the decision that changed everything between her and Jackson. This was not a man you fucked. This was the kind of man you honored, respected, and admired. A man you did not risk losing to satisfy some silly desire.

She would never sleep with Jackson King.

CHAPTER 4

NOW

*C*amille took his arm to walk down the aisle and Jackson flashed to a fantasy of the two of them at their own wedding. But she happened to be in a dark red dress, not a white one, and they were merely a bridesmaid and groomsman. And she was clearly furious with him.

She was so beautiful, it hurt him to look at her. He'd been studying her for a decade, and she'd become as integral to him as his arm or leg. He had never experienced anything like the relationship they'd built, and had never been so honest with another human being, even the siblings he adored.

It had always been different with Camille. Even from the beginning, she was one of the very few who saw underneath the intricate persona he created. Their connection was beyond friendship or attraction. It was a soul to soul connection that all of his analytical training could not understand but his heart knew to be true.

He could not pinpoint the moment he understood the nature of his feelings for her, as if they had always been. They were young when they first met and she was so fragile. Traumatized by her parents' death and completely inexperienced. He couldn't possibly have taken her the way he wanted. But it had been ten years, and she had turned out to be stronger and more capable than anyone he knew.

Their accidental kiss was his freedom from the faceless women he carried on his arm, from watching her love anyone else, from the arbitrary boundary that defined them as friends and not lovers.

They stepped in perfect rhythm, as instructed, greeting the large crowd around them, and pacing their movements to match the music. "You should never be a bridesmaid, Camille."

Her head tilted to search his face.

"You outshine every woman in this room. Including the bride."

She spoke through the perma-smile that she was forced to make as she met the happy eyes on either side of the aisle. "I'm begging you, Jackson. Please stop. I need to get through this wedding without falling apart."

He squeezed the hand tucked into his arm. "I just want you to know that I see you. I always have."

Something in the bottom of her abdomen made a gentle flip up to her heart when Jackson put his arm out for her as they entered the chapel. This man, who had always been her ideal, had made a case for a shift in their relationship. Of course she loved him. Of course she wanted him. He was the most important person in her life. That wasn't the point. Camille desperately wanted her best friend to resume that prized position and stop trying to fit himself in a more complicated way. There was too much at risk.

She sighed with relief as they moved to opposite sides of the altar. Her body still shimmered with the memory of his touch. It didn't help that he was gorgeous in his groomsman tux, either. As if God had designed the tuxedo for that particular man.

Their exit from the chapel was much easier, partially due to the ability to walk at a normal speed, and partially due to cheers and applause that greeted the entire wedding party. As soon as they were through the double doors, Camille unhooked from his arm and made her way to the bathroom to freshen up before the pictures.

Smiling and making nice for the camera were going to test every bit of her discipline and willpower. Her head was spinning, her heart was pounding, and her thoughts were everywhere she did not want them to be. How could she stand next to him and not get lost in the sensation of his body and her body almost…?

THE WEDDING PARTY and all family members waited outside the reception hall until all four hundred guests were seated. Keeping with tradition, each couple in the wedding party, as well as all immediate family members, would be introduced and make a choreographed entrance. Despite Camille's desire to put some space between herself and Jackson, she had been forced to be in close proximity to him all day. She looked everywhere but in his direction. Which is why she noticed the commotion in the lobby.

One particular woman was impossible to miss. The nearly six-foot frame, with legs that didn't stop, enormous breasts and a megawatt smile belonged to none other than Anya, Jackson's allegedly not-serious girlfriend who was not supposed to be there. But she was, entourage and all.

"You must be kidding."

Jackson followed the direction of her gaze. "What the…"

The line of his jaw hardened and his eyes burned. He spun on his heel and strode in Anya's direction. Camille recognized that expression, and that determined walk, and was glad not to be on the receiving end of what was coming.

Anya noticed him only after he was nearly on top of her. A

heart-melting smile covered her face as she wrapped her body around his.

"Hello my daahrling!"

Camille couldn't hear his response, but his body language was loud and clear. He did not hug her back. The expression on Anya's face didn't shift one bit. In fact, she took his face and kissed him. As if she were watching a train wreck, Camille could not pull away. That mouth, which had, mere hours ago, been on her own, was being possessed by another woman. They stayed connected for long enough that the entire wedding party began to notice. Little by little the whispers, giggles and excited comments filled the space. After all, Anya was most men's fantasy. Maybe some women's too.

By the time he finally broke away, Camille had had enough and turned her back to the scene. She had no right to feel the way she did, but betrayal seethed through her veins. This was exactly what she expected from their transgression. This was the nightmare she had successfully avoided all these years.

"AND NOW, we welcome Dr. Jackson King and Ms. Camille Moreau!!"

The applause tumbled out of the large room, but Camille had no companion. Uncertain what to do, she stepped through the door by herself. Jackson caught her around the waist just in time and they strode in together, stopping at the center of the dance-floor to wave, and then move directly to their table, just off to the right.

Camille jerked away from him as soon as the crowd's attention shifted to the next couple.

"Cam." He had his *don't mess with me* look on his face.

She would not be intimidated by him. "Don't. Just don't."

"I know you're upset. She said she wasn't coming. I don't know what happened. None of this was planned."

Camille forced herself to swallow the scathing words that

wanted to come flying out of her mouth. She knew she was over-reacting. She also knew this man could decipher every one of her expressions and emotions. "I'm fine, Jack. Your girlfriend has every right to be here. It was just… unexpected… that's all."

"Really, Cam? Are we resorting to bullshit now?"

Anya tackled him from behind. "Daaahrling, you keep running away from me!"

"Anya," he growled.

"Oh, hey, Camille. You don't mind my taking my boy, do you?" Without waiting for an answer, Anya pulled Jackson out to the dance-floor. When he turned back toward her, Camille looked away, forcing herself to focus on the silver vase in the middle of the table instead of the dread that pushed against her throat.

CAMILLE HAD JUST FINISHED CLEANING up her smeared eyeliner when Jenna came into the bathroom.

"Cam… what's wrong?"

She was no match for those clear blue eyes. "Something really bad has happened, Jenna. Really bad." The tears began again.

"Is this about Charlie? Because we can-"

"It's not about Charlie. It's about… "

"Jack."

Camille's hand froze in front of her face. "How did you know?"

"What happened with you two? What's going on?"

Camille looked down, away from the mirror, to collect her thoughts. She had to tell the truth. "We… almost slept together."

Jenna's face turned into a series of widening circles. "No fucking way."

"I can't believe, after all these years, we could screw up like that."

Jenna put her hands on Camille's shoulders. "Wait a minute. What happened? Exactly?"

"You don't want to hear this."

"You bet your ass I do. Just pretend we're not talking about my brother. It's just some guy you're telling me about."

The combination of too much champagne and desperation fueled Camille's honesty. "First he kissed me. Then he told me he loved me. Then-"

"Of course he loves you. You are like our-"

"No, Jenna. He told me he *loves* me."

The surprise in Jenna's expression passed so quickly, Camille nearly missed it. "I knew that, too."

Camille tilted her head to examine the face of the woman who was more like a sister than a friend, but who apparently knew more than she had ever said.

"He's been in love with you for a long time. But he was waiting for you."

Camille flushed. "I don't understand."

"I know. My brother - the most eligible bachelor on two coasts - has been pining for you forever. I'm not sure why he made his move now, with everything going on. Maybe he couldn't wait any longer." Jenna wiped a tear rolling toward Camille's ear. "Cam, I can't imagine what you must be feeling. So many ups and downs this weekend. But please know this: he is in love with you. I know my brother, and I would tell any woman on the planet to run, not walk, in the opposite direction. Except for you. You're the only one who makes him... normal. Like the man I know."

"This makes no sense, Jenna. He's out there right now with his girlfriend."

Jenna curled her lip. "You mean Anya? Be serious. She means nothing to him. He's humoring her so she doesn't make a scene. I don't think she's even into guys. She's just using him to get press attention." Jenna turned back to the mirror and ran a finger below her lower lip, removing any excess lipstick. "Listen, I'm not saying you need to be with him. I'm just saying that whatever he said, and whatever happened between you, it was real. There are no games when it comes to you."

Camille desperately wanted to ask her friend what to do. How to go back out into the party and watch him with another woman, whether it was pretend or not. She held her tongue.

Jenna moved toward the door. "Come on. Let's go back out there and enjoy this million dollar wedding."

"I'll be out in a sec."

Camille sighed at the sight of her red eyes and puffy face in the mirror. She would have to do something to take attention away from the remnants of her upset. One by one, she pulled each of the numerous bobby pins from her hair, releasing it from the elaborate updo. It was late enough in the reception that she was sure the bride wouldn't mind her breaking the dress code. The unleashing of her long auburn waves lessened the tension around her temples, and she forced herself to smile.

Jenna was right. It would be a shame to waste this extraordinary wedding fretting about nothing. Jackson had not promised her anything. She had no right to be upset. Besides, there were so many reasons it would be a bad idea to succumb to her feelings for Jackson. If only she could think of one.

She pushed open the door to find him standing directly in front of her.

"What are you doing, Jack?"

His expression was inscrutable. "I'm waiting for you."

"Why?"

"Because you promised me a dance. And I'm here to collect." A smile began to peek through.

Camille looked around to his left, toward the ballroom. "Where's Anya?"

"It doesn't matter."

Camille's face contorted in disapproval.

"Cam, I'm sorry. I had no idea she would show up even though I asked her not to. There's nothing happening between us. It's all for show. She's an actress, remember. You're the only one I'm concerned about tonight."

"Nothing has happened between us. But just the hint of it has created so much mess. At least for me. How can that be a good thing?"

"Growing into something is never comfortable."

She shook her head. "Don't psycho-babble me, please."

He lifted his chin in defense, then burst into a broad smile. "You realize you're the only one in my life I would allow to speak to me that way."

"That doesn't sound like something I should be concerned about."

He wrapped his finger around a curl of her hair. "Let's dance."

"Fine."

With all their friends celebrating in front of them, and his hand against her low back as they walked into the main hall, Camille had trouble remembering what she was supposed to be upset about.

How many songs had she danced with Jackson? Too many to count. Yet, when he pulled her to him, when their bodies pressed together, synchronized in movement, it was an altogether different experience than anything that had come before.

His face hovered inches away from hers. "I want to kiss you, Camille."

"You can't."

"I could, actually."

"But you won't."

"Why not?"

"Because your girlfriend is here, and all our friends are here, and nobody is ready for us to be kissing." *Least of all, me.*

He shook his head. "She's not my girlfriend. And I have never known you to give a shit about what anybody else thinks. Why start now?"

"Because we are attending a good friend's wedding, and we are considerate people, and we don't need to make a scene."

He raised an eyebrow. "You think my kisses are so good, there would be a scene?"

She rolled her eyes at him, which barely concealed the fact that what he said was true. "You exhaust me, Jackson."

"That's not quite the emotional response I was looking for, but it's better than anger. Or disdain."

"How do you know I'm not angry? Furious, even?"

A wide grin erupted across his face. "Because I've been studying you for ten years, love. And I am the expert in everything Camille."

She gave him a mock scowl. "Your humility is overwhelming, Dr. King."

"You're right. That was an overstatement."

Camille nearly tripped over her own feet at the rare appearance of Jackson admitting he had gotten something wrong.

"Steady there, girl. I'd love for you to fall all over me, but you just said this wasn't the time or place."

All she could do was sigh. "So, what correction would you like to make?"

"I am the expert in Camille the friend, but I have no experience of Camille the lover. Except secondhand, of course. I would imagine there are some significant differences."

All that smartness was wearing her down. "Such as?"

"Hmmm... good question. My initial thoughts would be that both emotional breadth and intensity would increase." He pulled back enough to make sure she could see his face. "And I greatly look forward to experiencing all of that. Every single laugh and cry and scream and moan."

She could not keep her face composed enough to pretend that his statement did not send tremors down the length of her body.

· · ·

AFTER THE MAIN RECEPTION, and two different after-parties, Camille was done. Jackson had not been more than a few feet away from her since their first dance, and he continued to follow her up to her room.

"I haven't invited you to stay with me."

"Not in words, no. But I'm staying." This man had enough confidence and certainty for three men.

"Jackson, you seem to think that I am eighteen again, and you are the wise older brother, or the boss. Those days are long gone."

"No one is happier about that than I am. You were no match for me back then. But now…" His eyes shimmered.

Her vision tunneled in on his mouth. His luscious, beautiful mouth. All those years of resisting dissolved in a single impulse. She tipped forward and kissed him. As soon as their lips touched, he responded by pulling her tightly to him. Her hands wove into his hair, his hands slid down her back, coming to rest at the curve of her bottom. His tongue parted her lips and explored her mouth. She arched her back, pushing her breasts into his chest. He squeezed a handful of her ass.

She pulled away to catch her breath.

"Open the door, Camille."

The inferno in her body easily drowned out the warning whispers in her head.

Even before the door had latched shut, she slipped her hands under his lapels and pushed his jacket off. While he buried his mouth in her neck, she pulled the bottom of his shirt out of his pants and unbuttoned it. The top half of his body was bare in moments and her hands took full advantage.

"You feel as good as you look, Jack." She skimmed her hands over the angles of his chest, the ridges of his abdomen, and the curves of his arms. Then she followed with her mouth, giving one of his small, tight nipples a lick. A groan escaped on his breath.

The bulge in his pants demanded her attention next, and

away went his pants, shoes, and underwear. She was fully dressed, he was stripped bare. This was just about the right balance of power for her.

"Do you like what you see, love?" He gave his cock a slow stroke and she had to bite her lip not to gasp. She moved his hand away and took over, wrapping her fingers around him and sliding from head to base. The rumors were true. Jackson King was seriously well endowed.

"Aaah." His groan resounded directly into her body.

She needed his mouth so she moved in for another kiss while keeping him in her hand.

His fingers fumbled on her back, and she realized he was unzipping her dress. Once the zipper reached her waist, the swath of crimson fabric fell away, creating a pool at her feet. She was left in only the bustier they all had specially made to fit under the strapless bridesmaid dresses, her nearly invisible lace thong, and a pair of camel colored stilettos.

This package was not lost on the man before her. "Holy shit, Camille. You are... killing me..." His thumb skimmed across the top of her pushed-up breasts, then dropped the front cup of the bustier to pinch her dark rose nipple. The next second, it became the pull of his mouth and the scrape of his teeth. She reached for his shoulders as her balance faltered.

When he lifted his head to look at her, she swallowed, remembering the vow she'd made and the line she never expected to cross.

He took her hand, led her to the bed, sat down, and brought her onto his lap. His erection pressed against her hip and she wondered if he could feel her wetness on his thigh.

"Talk to me, Cam. What's going on? You look..." He pursed his lips.

"I just didn't expect to ever be like this... with you. Isn't it a shock for you, to see me like this?"

He shook his head for too long before speaking. "I always knew we would be together. Like this."

Her stomach dropped to the bottom of her torso, out onto the floor, and down the nine stories to the lobby of the hotel. Never in a million years did she expect that the man she trusted like family had set his sights on nailing her. She was another conquest. Her whole body shook.

"Does that scare you, love? You look frightened." He took her face in his hands. "Cam. Say something. I don't know what you're thinking. I don't know what that expression means."

She pushed herself off his lap and onto her feet. "I thought you were the expert in Camille."

A fire consumed her chest and throat. It was impossible to breathe deeply enough to calm herself down.

He stood up and clutched her arms. "Camille, what's going on right now? Whatever you're thinking, whatever is making you this angry, it can be explained. Please don't pull away from me like this."

"Get out of my room."

"I'm not leaving until you tell me what's wrong. What just happened?"

"Jackson, please understand me when I say that it would be in your best interest to get as far away from me as possible. I'm going into the bathroom right now. Get dressed and be gone by the time I come out." She stepped out of her shoes and strode into the bathroom. Without bothering to turn the light on, she sat on the edge of the cold bathtub.

Jenna said he'd been in love with her for years. But she was wrong. He just wanted to screw her. All that restraint she'd shown over all these years and he would happily throw it all away for a roll in the sack. Rustling from the room pulled her attention to the bathroom door. He wouldn't dare enter.

A few minutes later the front door latched and she made her way back into the room, into bed, and buried herself under a mountain of blankets.

CHAPTER 5

SIX YEARS EARLIER

*J*ackson rearranged the fabric around his neck. The doctoral sash was too garish, in his opinion. But it definitely made it clear he was receiving an important degree.

It had only been five years since graduating from college. He smiled as he remembered fussing with his graduation cap, trying to figure out how to get it to stay on his unruly mass of thick hair. Of course his father had admonished him to get a haircut, which would have helped, but he would never have admitted it.

He'd been so excited to begin his life as an adult. It was going to be goodbye California, goodbye Dad, hello New York. Staying close to home during college had been a compromise to his worried parents. Maybe it had been the wrong decision, but choosing Columbia University for his doctorate was the perfect remedy. Nothing like the whole United States to put some distance between him and his overbearing family.

Jackson's college graduation had been anticlimactic. Sure,

his mother had gone all out, renting the fanciest restaurant in town and inviting all his friends and their families. But, as predicted, his father just couldn't bear to make Jackson the center of attention. All the trouble Jackson had gotten in certainly didn't help. But that was so long ago. No need to delve into all that mess again.

He was about to officially receive a PhD. Dr. Jackson King had a great ring to it and put on a grin on his face. He smoothed his palms down the satin fabric one more time before walking out to the reception area with his fellow graduates, who scattered to find their loved ones. Fathers were clutching shoulders, mothers were crying. Beaming, blue-robed graduates gathered with their congratulatory families and headed off to their respective celebrations.

He scanned the small crowd for his family. Jonathan King was unmistakable, debonair in his dark suit, standing a head above anyone else. Their physical similarities were undeniable, as was their ability to command a room.

Very little was said as the whole family made their way through the crowd toward the packed parking structure. No matter how many times he explained to his parents that a car in New York City was nothing but an inconvenience, they just couldn't let go of their California habits. Thank goodness the city was slightly quieter than usual on that cloudy Sunday afternoon.

Jackson and his family walked through the restaurant his mother had chosen, on a different coast than the one years ago, but otherwise indistinguishable. It felt like deja vu when his father raised a glass. Jackson could almost recite the toast from his college graduation, word for word.

"We have so much to celebrate this fine day. Let's offer a toast to Julian and Jackson! We send Julian off to UCLA to change the face of computer science, and we wish Jackson lots of luck in New York City." Jonathan had turned toward his son with an expression free from irony. "He'll need it."

Maybe his father would try to contain his disdain this time around. Probably not. It wasn't news that his father didn't agree with his line of study. It had been a hard decision to veer away from engineering to go into the soft sciences. Jonathan King did not consider psychology a science at all. It was something that people with too much time on their hands did to feel important. Just one of many ways Jackson had failed his father.

The significant difference this time around was the presence of the wonderful woman standing next to him. Camille was a part of their family now, and maybe, with her there, it would be better. He reached down and took her hand, which she gave an excited squeeze.

"Cheers!" All the glasses met in the center of the table for a cascade of clinks.

Jonathan cleared his throat, making sure all attention was on him. "We are fortunate on so many levels. My wonderful girls, Jenna and Camille, successfully graduating from Princeton, the alma mater of my beloved Elena. Off to conquer Silicon Valley and the dastardly world of politics. We wish them all the success they have worked so hard to deserve."

Glasses touched and Jonathan waited for full silence to begin again.

"And of course, to Jackson and his continued academic successes. Hopefully, he won't let getting called doctor King go to his head and actually attempt to operate on anyone!" Jonathan's bellowing laugh completely covered the uncomfortable titter around him.

Elena King raised her glass. "And thank you to Princeton and Columbia for holding their graduations on the same weekend, but not the same day! I just don't know how we would have managed!"

Jackson knew exactly whose graduation would have been given short shrift.

The celebration moved to Jackson's loft, where it shifted in tone and doubled in size. He'd made a huge number of friends during his time in New York, and his place was bursting with an assortment of people as varied as the city's population.

Jackson sat on the couch, surveying the wonder of his life in New York. This was exactly what he intended when he chose to begin in a new place. His goal had been to build something completely on his own, outside the reaches of his powerful family. Being in a community was very important to him, and he wanted his own.

He stretched out his arm and signaled to Camille to join him. She plopped down, snuggling into the side of his body. They were Camnjack - the two-headed, single-named entity, well known to everyone around them. They'd both recently dispensed with their respective love interests, knowing those relationships would never survive the cross-country move. There was no one to get jealous about their closeness.

"Another great party, Jackson. Epic."

He squeezed her shoulder. "Thanks, Cam."

He looked out at the city skyline and felt a tinge of sadness about leaving.

"Are you feeling melancholy already?"

"Yeah. I'm going to miss this place, this city, the life I built here. It's been remarkable."

She nodded, a tendril of hair coming loose from the place behind her ear she constantly pushed it. "Well, a brand new, even better life awaits you back in California. As Professor King of Stanford University. I can't believe you're going to be molding young minds. Scary. Very scary."

"Thankfully they won't be that young. And I did pretty well molding your young mind. I mean, look at you now." Look at her indeed, outshining every woman in the room. She had metamorphosed from the tentative girl he nearly knocked over the first day they met to a bold, confident, brilliant woman who was going to own Silicon Valley before too long. She certainly owned him.

"Really? You think you molded me?" She poked him in the ribs.

"Wishful thinking on my part." He glanced down, then blinked at the curve of her breast directly in his sightline.

"Personally, I'm glad we're moving back. We have great jobs, an amazing house, and no more snow. It's going to be so much fun living with you and Jenna. The three amigos take the Bay!"

He tilted his head toward her, being careful to not look down at the enticing view below. "You mean Camnjack plus Jenna."

"You better stop saying that. You know how mad she gets when she feels left out."

"Hey, she's the one who made up Camnjack."

"True enough. But you better embed the three amigos in that big brain of yours."

He gave her a sly smile. "You think my brain is big? You should see my-"

That merited a punch in the thigh. "Don't be lewd, Jackson. Seriously."

He had never had a relationship like the one he built with Camille. She was the best of all worlds for him - the buddy who could hang out and drink beer, the babe who made every man look, and the friend whose loyalty was only outmatched by her kindness. Their conversations flowed from school, to sex, to sports and everything in between without a hitch or hiccup.

He watched her as her eyes flitted around the room. She might not have even known how big a smile was plastered on her face. It had been four years of going to her when he struggled with a decision, teaching her how to dance, and saving him a hundred times from quitting his doctoral program.

Her fingers picked at the frayed section of his jeans near his knee. She'd given him the confidence to write his book, while he'd given her the lowdown on men and sex, including the practice run putting condoms on bananas. Jackson was never happier than when she laughed so hard she fell into his arms, and never more uncomfortable than when his desire caught him by surprise and could not be suppressed. She'd been a beautiful girl, but the woman she had grown into brought him to his knees.

He didn't blame anyone for giving them shit about how inseparable they were. He had no interest in being apart from her.

Two of his neighbors walked by them and waved, in an attempt at a conga line, he believed. Living in the same household was going to be trickier, but worth it. Keeping himself out of her bedroom was going to take all the self-discipline he could muster. Maybe more. Crossing the line, however, was not an option. This odd relationship they had built was the best thing in his life, and he wasn't about to jeopardize it for a twitch in his pants.

He accidentally looked down her shirt again and clenched his jaw. He imagined the number of women he would need to distract himself from the one he really wanted. It was a big number.

CAMILLE STUMBLED out into the living room in a desperate quest for coffee. She usually loved this house. Jackson had chosen well. It was beautiful, spacious, and conveniently located. But it was not soundproof. They all had serious jobs, but Jackson was still living the life of a party animal, as evidenced that morning by a pink lace bra hanging off the kitchen countertop. It did not belong to any of the house's occupants. Camille gritted her teeth, picked up the offending item with the end of a wooden spoon, and tossed it into the living room.

Her decision to move in with Jackson had been a big mistake. The stream of scantily clad women coming and going in their house was more than she could handle. She and Jackson were the best of friends, but being this close to his extraordinary sex habits was wrecking her life. Since Jenna had started spending all her time with her new boyfriend, there was no one to serve as a buffer.

By the time she was halfway through her mug of coffee, Camille had made a decision. She could easily afford her own place and was going to move out. She opened her laptop to a rental website and input her criteria.

The first one to emerge out of Jackson's room was a naked redhead, presumably looking for the bathroom. He came out clothed, thankfully, minutes later.

"Hey Cam. How was your night?"

Instead of an answer, she tilted her head and squinted her eyes at him. Was he not aware how thin the walls were?

"Oh. Sorry." He grimaced. "What are you up to today?"

A voice interrupted Camille's answer. "Has anybody seen my bra? It's pink and-"

Without looking up, afraid to get another eyeful, Camille answered. "It's on the floor by the couch."

"Thanks, hun."

Could this be any worse? Camille picked up her mug and computer, and headed into her bedroom, which shared a wall with Jackson's room, but would hopefully be quiet now that his guest was getting dressed.

She had bookmarked more than a dozen possible places and was pleased that there was quite a bit available in her price range. Her parents had left her a significant estate, but Camille was never one for unnecessary extravagance.

The knock on her door was followed by his voice. "Hey, Cam. Can I come in?"

She said yes, not that she really had a choice.

"I made another pot of coffee, just the way you like it. I brought you some." He held out the light blue mug with a drawing of the Eiffel Tower that he had bought for her.

The tension around her jaw softened. "Thanks."

He put it down on the night table and sat down on the bed next to her.

"What are you up to?" His slight smile was more concerned than happy.

"Actually, I'm looking for an apartment."

It was as if all the blood drained from his face, emphasizing his dark eyes and hair even more. He did not look happy. "You're moving out? No, please don't. I'm sorry about this morning. And last night. Please don't go."

"It's not just today. It's every weekend. And sometimes during the week too. This is where I live, and I never know who's going to be here. And whether they'll be dressed or not. I need something more… stable."

"Cammy…" He pressed his lips together before continuing. "I'm sorry. I don't want you to go. You're my best friend. I love living with you."

"We're not going to be best friends much longer if I stay here. I'm not happy."

"What would make you happy?"

Something about the look in his eyes broadcast trouble. He might have spent the night fucking, but he seemed to be looking at her like he wanted more.

"I'm going to go. Things will be better after that. I'm sure of it."

He balled the edge of her sheet in his fist. "Is there anything I can do?"

"You can go take a shower. You smell like pussy."

His mouth dropped open, as if he had been punched in the gut, and then he walked out of her room.

~

JACKSON STARTED DRINKING VERY EARLY on the day Camille moved out, making it impossible for him to help. Not that she had asked.

Things had been strained since that morning she told him she was going to leave. He knew it was one hundred percent his fault, parading all those girls in and out of the house, desperately trying to compensate for the one he wanted but couldn't have.

She left without saying goodbye. They didn't speak for two months.

He was supposed to be by her side, and now she couldn't stand to be around him. He could hardly stand it himself. All the attention he had been getting for his books was turning him into a monster. And she was the only one who reminded him of his better self. He would have to find a way to bring her back, to show her how much he loved her without scaring her away. He knew she didn't see him that way. In fact she recoiled at any hint of his feelings for her. But he couldn't live without her. So having her as a best friend instead of the love of his life would have to do.

He left the meeting with his editor dejected and desperate. The new book just wasn't working and would require a complete rewrite. The publisher had already extended the deadline once and wasn't likely to do it again. Not thinking, he drove south and found himself in the large parking lot of the Google campus. It could not have been more inappropriate to ambush Camille at work, but he couldn't stand one more day without her.

No one stopped him as he strode into the center of the large expanse of cubicles and then toward her office to the far right. Perhaps the determination of his expression was enough to dissuade any interruption in his path.

A spectrum of emotions transformed her face as she watched him approach her glass-walled office. She popped up out of her chair, eyes wild with... was it fear, relief, confusion?

He opened the door, stepped in and began speaking immediately, not allowing anything to stop him from saying what he came to say. "Hi, Camille. I'm sorry to barge in on you at work.

I know you're very busy. I needed to talk to you, to see you, and it felt impossible to wait even one more minute."

He took a breath and she sat back down, wordless. He continued. "I'm here because... The reason I'm here is..." He had to swallow a swell of emotion clogging his throat. Why was this so hard? "What I came here to say is I love you, and I miss you, and I'm sorry I was such an asshat that you were forced out of your own home.

"I understand if you don't want to live with me anymore, but I can't not have you in my life. It just doesn't work without you in it, Camille. So, will you please forgive me? Please take me back."

She picked at the nail of her left thumb, the habit he had long known signaled discomfort. After a painful pause, she pushed her chair back, stood up, and walked toward him. They stood face to face as she examined him, and he became even more uncomfortable under her scrutinizing gaze. He wasn't sure whether she was going to scream, or hit him, or something worse. Instead, she put her arms underneath his and hugged him tightly.

"I love you too, Jack. I never stopped being your friend."

The juxtaposition of the two statements caused a searing pain in his chest. Although the former was music to his ears, the latter was devastating.

CHAPTER 6

NOW

$\mathcal{T}$he plane touched down in a foggy San Francisco. Camille was relieved to have left behind all the drama of Chicago, the wedding, and the emotional ruckus created by her now ex-boyfriend and her best friend, whose status was currently undetermined. All the energy she required to make it home left her drained and shaky. She didn't worry about unpacking, preparing for work the next day, or checking mail.

She took an indulgent shower until there was no more hot water and then crawled into bed. The fact that it was the middle of the afternoon bore no relevance to her decision.

She wasn't surprised to wake up at eleven pm, starving and disoriented. This was going to screw her up for at least a day, maybe two. While the soup warmed on the stovetop, she picked up her phone, which had been curiously silent since she'd left Chicago. The lack of activity was not only unexpected, it was nearly impossible considering the shitstorm she'd left behind.

The tiny airplane in the upper left corner explained the lack of incoming communication. Like opening an overfull cabinet, switching her phone off of airplane mode resulted in a cascade of rings, pings, and buzzes while her screen filled with every type of message bubble available. She poured the soup into a broad patterned bowl and carried it, along with her phone, to the dining table. Waiting for the soup to cool enough provided the perfect window to tally the goings on of the past few hours.

Nearly all the activity on her phone came from Jackson, and perhaps the rest was related to him as well. Instead of taking the time to start from the beginning, Camille opened the most recent texts and voicemails. Listening to his strained voice clenched the base of her throat. He spoke with the controlled anger she had seen him use with his father during their epic disagreements.

"We are not doing this, Camille. Not again. I can accept that I probably fucked up, even though I still don't know exactly how. What I can't accept is you shutting me out. Regardless of what happened this weekend, you are still the most important person in my life. I'll be coming back from the east coast on Monday night and I'm going straight to your apartment. Please be there."

She listened to his voicemail three times and then stopped herself from any more replays by deleting the message. Ever since she realized that the world was not going to hand her everything she wanted, and in fact would more often hand her exactly what she didn't want, Camille had become adept at saying no, and meaning it. The exception was the tall man with the square jaw, ebony hair and milk chocolate eyes whom she had found nearly impossible to refuse. The conversation she would have with him in less than 24 hours was going to be the ultimate test of her ability.

~

WHEN SHE OPENED the door to him, the first thing that struck her was that the consistently photo-ready Jackson King was a mess. His hair was disheveled, his eyes were ringed with dark circles, and his jacket had a yellow stain near the lapel.

"Thank you for agreeing to this." Fatigue flowed from his words.

She swallowed a snarky comment about her clear lack of agreement. "I'm not sure what you expect."

He walked into the kitchen and poured himself a glass of water. "I'm sorry, Cam. I don't know what I did, but I know something upset you. And under those circumstances…"

The spot between Camille's eyebrows tightened. "What circumstances?"

"We were naked, Camille. At least I was. We were being intimate. To have a boundary crossed in that situation is especially traumatic. So I sincerely and completely apologize."

"To apologize for something you don't even know seems completely disingenuous."

He pressed his hand to his forehead. "No, it's not disingenuous. It's love. You see, I don't need to know what I did so that I can defend it or justify it. I just know that it upset you, and I never want that, and so that's enough for me to proclaim that I'm sorry it happened."

"So you don't care to know what happened?"

He slammed the glass down so hard it startled them both. "Goddammit, Camille please don't twist words to escalate this thing. I'm trying my best here."

She took the few steps to the couch and sat down, still shaky from the explosive outburst. "You said something… it scared the shit out of me."

He sat down next to her, but far enough away not to encroach on her space. "What did I say? And why did it scare you?"

She picked at her thumbnail. "We were talking about how

odd it was to be broaching a different type of intimacy. Well, I thought it was odd. And you said you always knew it was going to happen."

He took a drawn-out breath, as if he was inhaling recognition and understanding. "Holy shit."

"What I heard was that while I was respecting you and our relationship, deliberately choosing not to become one of your fuck-buddies, you were doing the opposite. Just biding your time."

"Oh my God, Cam. I…" He shook his head and groaned. "Is that still what you believe?" His eyes were dissolving her resolve.

"Maybe. Maybe not. I'm going to give you the benefit that you might have meant it another way than my interpretation."

In one swift move, he brought his body beside her. He took the thumb she had been fidgeting with and brought it to his lips. "Oh, Cam. I can't believe you thought I would ever be so cruel or callous. That's not who we are to each other, love. I have messed up more than my share, but I would never say something like that to you."

"Then what did you mean?"

His lips brushed against the back of her hand, then her wrist. "What I meant is that I knew we would be together. In love and in relationship. Even all those years you kept rejecting me."

He had gone too far. "What are you talking about, Jackson? I have never once rejected you in my entire life."

"Camille, you let me into your heart, yes. You let me into your most personal and private thoughts. But not as a man. As a platonic friend. And whenever I expressed anything that had the slightest hint of romantic desire, your walls went up so fast, they nearly knocked me down. For years, this was how it worked with us. I had to conceal that part of my feelings for you, for fear that you would entirely shut me out."

While her head tried to process the string of revelations

coming out of his mouth, Camille's heart spun and leapt and pounded. She could not admit that all those years she had completely misunderstood his motives. "That's not true."

"Think about it. Remember, when you moved out of our house? Remember when we went to the awards gala, which you refused to acknowledge as a date, and then you called me a man-whore? I've got so many more examples, too."

"Wait a minute." Camille could see each of those scenes so clearly, but now they were tainted by a conflicting perspective. She struggled to realign the situation as she had understood it for so long. "But you didn't try anything."

"Yes, well... I realized that, for whatever reason, you weren't going to go there with me. So, I put all those thoughts and desires away for a later day."

"And then Friday." The day of their first kiss.

"And then Friday."

"But why then?"

"When I saw you sobbing on the floor, something snapped. I couldn't watch you mistreated by yet another jackass. You were supposed to be with *me*, Camille. And I guess everything that I had kept so tightly buried came pouring out. You needed to know... No, it's not that you needed to know. It's that I needed to say it. To admit it. Honestly and out loud. No more hiding."

A soft sigh of understanding floated out of her. His version of the story made so much more sense. Why had she gotten so caught up in such a hurtful viewpoint?

"Those moments with you were... extraordinary. I mean, we only had the smallest taste of what it would be like to be with each other in that way. And it was amazing, Camille."

She dropped her head onto his shoulder. She couldn't disagree. "I'm so tired, Jack. You and Charlie messed me up this weekend."

"I know. It wasn't particularly fair to you. And for that I'm sorry."

"I'm sorry too. For misreading your actions."

He gently moved her off his shoulder to look into her eyes. "Are we okay, Cam? Do you feel resolved about what happened?"

She didn't like it when he used his psychology voice, but she was too tired to argue. "Yes, Jack."

"What would you like the next step to be?"

"I want to go to bed."

He bobbed his head in agreement.

"And I want you to come with me."

The nodding became a wide smile.

CAMILLE DOZED off when he was in the shower, but woke up as he snuggled himself behind her.

When she reached around to touch him, her palm was greeted with his bare bottom.

"Are you naked, Jackson?"

"Yes. Is that a problem?"

There was no possible argument she could muster. "Goodnight."

"Goodnight, love."

SHE WATCHED HIM SLEEP. There was just enough light in the room for her to make out his features. The square jaw, strong brow, deep set eyes and the small scar on his nose from the bar fight all softened when he slept. She moved her face only the few inches to press her lips onto his. He responded immediately, wrapping his arm so tightly around her that she gasped.

"Camille." The gravel of his sleep-filled voice rumbled directly between her legs. "Tell me what you want."

"I want to know how it feels."

His mouth moved to her neck. "How what feels?"

"How it feels to have you love me… like this."

He lifted his head from her body, paused and then leaned back to see her face. "I need you to be explicit, Camille."

His quick shift from groggy to dead serious put a flutter in her breath. "I want to be with you, Jackson. Physically."

"Mmmm…"

When he didn't move, she reached forward to kiss him again.

He pulled away. "Wait."

Camille thought she might die from self-consciousness.

"Don't freak out, Cam."

She hated how he could so easily read her. "I'm not…"

He brought his hand to her face and stroked her cheek. The tenderness began to soothe the tension. "Just hold on, love."

She matched her breathing to his.

"We've had two false starts, which ended pretty badly. At least for me. I'd rather not get kicked out of your room again."

"Ouch."

His thumb traced the outline of her lower lip. "I'm not trying to be hurtful, love."

She squeezed her eyes shut to organize her thoughts, too distracted by his face. And his finger. "You got into bed with me naked, Jack. I don't understand the hesitation now."

He nodded. "I can see how that seems inconsistent. There are a few different things going on. First, I never sleep with clothes on. And I wanted the experience of my body touching yours." He took a beat. "Also, I suppose part of me is trying to get you used to me here, like this. I think my new role, as more of a sexual presence, is triggering you. It's making you more sensitive and reactive than you normally would be. I thought if you could get used to me, physically, we could move forward more smoothly."

"That sounds very well thought out, Jackson. And not in a good way."

He laughed. "I love when you call me out, Cam. It's one of

my favorite things about you. Okay, my delivery aside, do you understand what I'm saying?"

"Yes, I understand all of it. And probably agree. Everything's felt sharper since... the kiss. It feels like I'm swinging between desire, terror, and grief."

"Wow. That sounds intense." He pulled her closer.

"I can feel your boner, Jack."

"Sorry. Actually, not sorry. But I am listening to you, Camille. In addition to wanting you."

"Fair enough."

He pulled himself slightly away. "Can we deconstruct this a bit?"

"Oooh, does this mean I'm getting a free session with the renowned Dr. King? Complete with hard-on?"

He wrinkled the center of his forehead. "Since you mock so freely, yes, you are."

"Excellent."

Jackson looked into her eyes. "Tell me about the desire part of your feelings."

"Seriously?"

"Yes."

It was too hard to have this discussion so close to him. "Fine. I feel desire for you. Done."

"Not so fast, darlin'."

"Desire is the easy part, Jack. And it's not new. You are an amazing, attractive, wonderful man. Of course I want you. Can we move on?"

"You've said a few things that I didn't know, but, okay, we can move on. Tell me about terror."

"I'm terrified that this singular relationship we spent a decade building will be ruined. You are the most important person in my life and I've had a firsthand view of how women come and go in your life. I just couldn't take that."

An impermeable and utterly professional expression, the

one he'd been perfecting over all these years, took over his face. "Do you feel like you're going to lose me?"

She swallowed hard. This was not a conversation she wanted to have anywhere, much less in bed with him. "Obviously."

"Love is risky." A twitch crossed his left eye.

"Please don't give me a canned answer."

He exhaled. "There are no guarantees. But in terms of possibilities for success, ours is phenomenal. I don't consider our foray a mutually temporary arrangement. I'm not trying to go there for some passing desire or curiosity. I'm going there because I feel like our relationship is incomplete without this part."

"Compelling. And well thought out. Again."

He frowned. "I feel like you're mocking me. Again."

"No. But I am mirroring your professional tone."

"I know you don't want to talk about this-"

"No. I don't"

"But we need to. I understand after the trauma of losing your parents, it would seem unreasonable to risk losing someone else you care about."

That was the last straw. She separated their bodies. "Don't bring my parents into this."

Jackson moved the covers that had slipped off her bare chest back up under her chin, covering her up. "I'm sorry, love."

She curled her knees into her chest and closed her eyes, desperately hoping that Jackson would stop forcing her to talk about everything. When she blinked her eyes open, he was staring at her. It felt like pure love reflected in his eyes. Despite the anxiety creating a buzz in her body, she had to admit the improbability of harm. There was nowhere safer than with him.

He ran his hand lightly down the outside of her arm. Then up to her neck and shoulder. Then down her arm. Over and over, soothing her into sharing again.

"I'm scared." Her voice cracked. "The thought of getting our rocks off with each other, and blowing up something exceptional terrifies me."

"Me too."

She sucked in a sharp breath, never expecting that admission. "You too?"

"Of course, Cam. My life without you in it is unimaginable."

"So why are you willing to risk everything?"

She watched his shoulders rise and fall as he took several breaths.

"Because I want all of you. It's less a gamble and more like a necessary next step. But I haven't been through what you've been through. I understand that grief plays a greater role in your perspective than in mine."

She remembered saying one of her current emotions was grief. It had only been minutes, but felt like hours ago.

"Will you tell me about it?"

"I just got dumped, as you remember. And even though it was for the best, it was still an ending. And I feel grief about us. About the simplicity and ease of how we were. I'm not sure we could ever get that back." She decided against mentioning the grief that had been with her for for as long as she could remember.

"I can only speak for myself, but it was not simple or easy to hide my feelings from you. It's been messier since the kiss, but it feels better. At least I'm being honest. That's really important to me."

He had a point. "I hate how you have this all figured out. I don't."

"I don't either, love. And I honor everything you've told me. I don't want you to think I'm disregarding what you're feeling. I get all of it. And I wish I could take all the bad stuff away and make being with me nothing but pleasure and delight. It hurts me that you're hurting."

Camille considered her options. He was right. There was no

one on the planet better suited to her. If it was true that his relationship with her would not be anything like the string of women in and out of his life, then they would do well. But that was a big if.

"I have an idea, Cam. Most couples jumping into a sexual relationship don't know each other at all. But we know each other better than we know ourselves. And I don't trust anyone as much as I trust you. So I don't think we need to follow the traditional path. However, maybe some of it would be helpful."

"What do you mean?"

"Let's date."

That nearly blew a circuit in her brain. "Date?"

"Yes, like a normal couple getting to know each other."

"That sounds fine to me." She imagined romantic dinners, walking hand-in-hand in the city, car rides up to wine country. It all felt lovely. But going backwards to dating meant... "No sex, right?"

"I think that's a good idea."

She expected to be more surprised, or more disappointed than she was. Perhaps the proximity to his body was dulling the impact of what he was saying. "No more sleeping together naked, either."

"Well, I think that should continue."

Camille curled her lip. "Seriously?"

"And you will also be naked."

"Now I know you're joking."

"I told you it's not going to follow cultural norms. We have our own path, and that includes being in the same bed together. Unclothed."

It made no sense. "Why be naked if we're not having sex?"

"Because you need to get used to me. To redefine who I am to you."

"And you're going to be able to hold yourself back?" She doubted her own ability to contain her desire.

"I am. I give you my word, Cam. Not until it feels completely right for you."

Camille rolled onto her back and exhaled loudly. This was one of the unorthodox methods that had made Jackson a superstar in his field. She didn't doubt he knew what he was doing. Her body, however, had different ideas.

CHAPTER 7

NOW

"*D*on't get too dressed up. Things might get messy."

Where could Jackson possibly be taking her? For their first date, Camille had expected an elegant dinner. Maybe even dancing. Were they going to clean the streets or build houses?

It was sushi-making. A class at the local, and also world-renowned, culinary school, the California Culinary Academy.

Jackson had clearly put some effort into planning a week of fun adventures for their foray into dating. She wondered if he was feeling that same sense of heightened stakes. They were so close to getting what they'd both secretly wanted for so long. It felt like all or nothing.

When they arrived at her apartment, all the uncertainty rushed back in. It was easier to be with him than anyone else in her life. But the idea of getting back into bed with him scared her to bits.

He undressed first and got into bed buck naked, as he had informed her. When she tried wearing a t-shirt, he sat up.

"Cam, will you be naked with me?" Something about his expression wiped away any doubts from her mind. It was the honest, vulnerable man she recognized from their years together. She pulled off her shirt, then slid down her thong and slipped under the covers. He pulled her into him keeping his arms wrapped tight enough to mold their bodies together.

"How does this feel?"

So hard to form words. "Really good."

"Tell me specifically."

She pressed her forehead into the top of his chest and closed her eyes in an attempt to focus on coherence. "My skin is warm, my heart is beating really fast. My breasts are pushed against you, and it hurts a little."

He loosened his grip.

She took a deep breath. "I feel an ache between my legs, and your erection pressing against my thigh. When I realize it's you, and your body, it's disorienting, and I feel like I keep having to bring myself back. To be present."

"That's so good. Is there anything scaring you right now?"

"No. Well, maybe. It's more like anticipation. I want you."

"How do you want me?"

All those years of speaking so frankly with Jackson about sex had perfectly prepared her for that moment. "I want you to kiss me, and touch me, and be inside me. With your fingers and your mouth and your cock."

A rumble vibrated through his chest and out of his mouth. He tightened his grip around her.

"What are you feeling, Jack?"

"I'm feeling like I'm barely managing to keep my desire in control and not ravage you. My dick is so hard it hurts pretty bad. But my word to you is more important than any of that, so I'm not going to do anything."

"I don't understand. Why are we doing this?" The over-whelming sensations were clouding her memory of the decision they'd made.

"Because your desire for me is not yet integrated. It's clear in your body, but not yet in your mind, which could make you feel regretful. I want you to move through all of that until the dissonance passes. And I want you to want me."

"I do want you, Jackson."

"More."

COOL AND CASUAL, he'd told her in preparation for their next date. The taxi dropped them off at The Fillmore and she looked up at the marquee to see the name of her favorite local band. The one whose tickets were impossible to get.

"You didn't..."

He beamed as brightly as the neon signs. "I sure did."

"Amazing, Jack. Just amazing."

It didn't matter that it was so crowded, she could hardly breathe. It didn't matter that her eardrums had probably suffered permanent damage from the volume. All that mattered was their singing, dancing, and screaming for two straight hours.

When they went to bed, Camille didn't wait for him to come to her. She lunged for his mouth and wrapped her hand around his cock. It was a mad, feverish scramble to get as connected as possible. He did not resist.

Until he sprung from the bed, panting, erection raging in front of him, almost as if he'd heard an intruder. Without saying anything, he walked into the bathroom, turned on the shower, and stepped in. His groan echoed all the way into the bedroom.

When he returned, he slipped back into the bed and looked at her sheepishly. "Sorry, Cam. It was getting too much."

"I can't do this again, Jack. The logic keeps leaving me. I'm not feeling more grounded, I'm feeling less. Everything is too intense."

"Maybe this wasn't the right approach. I'm sorry."

She placed her palm on his chest, surprised to still feel the deep pounding. "Did the cold shower help?"

"A little. Not enough."

She moved her hand down his chest, over his abdomen, and gripped him tightly.

"Cam…" He moved her hand and held it, softly, away from both of their bodies.

They lingered in this limbo, connected by wide eyes, synchronized breath, and a single hand. Camille swore she could feel the beating of his heart across those few inches that separated their naked bodies. She arched her back, jutting her breasts toward him, aching for more connection.

He moved just outside of her reach. "Do you trust that I'm going to keep my promise to you, Camille?"

It was almost as if he was speaking in slow motion, the movement of his lips resonating inside her. She had no interest in the promise. "Yes."

He inched toward her, so close that the heat from his body was unmistakable. It was as if he was running his hands and mouth over every inch of her skin. But they were still separated, except for that hand and the steady warm breath enveloping her.

She closed her eyes and squeezed her thighs together, the imagined sensation of him everywhere in her and around her all of a sudden overwhelming. It couldn't be…

A wave of pleasure washed over her, followed by a deep groan that she could neither expect nor hold back. The next sensations were tightness in the fingers Jackson had interlaced with hers and something warm on her arm. She watched, breathless, as his face contorted and his breath stuttered.

He never broke eye contact with her. Never let go of her hand. Never touched her or himself.

Almost nothing that she experienced with Jackson was ordinary. But those few minutes, when he breathed both of them

COLLECTING SECRETS | 71

into climax, without even the slightest touch, was what the word extraordinary had been invented to describe.

$$\sim$$

THREE YEARS earlier

"Come with me, Cam." Jackson squeezed his hands into fists to hide the shaking. They had gotten past the rough patch when she moved out, but he still felt so unsteady around her.

"Me? Don't you have a ton of gala-ready girls who'd be better?"

He shook his head at the question. "Camille, this is a big deal for me. Maybe the most important night of my life. And it's because of you. There's no one I'd rather go with." Three years out of school, three books later, he had been selected as the youngest recipient of the Golden Pen Award for global impact from a piece of writing. To call it a big deal was a drastic understatement.

She touched her fingertips to his cheek, unaware of the storm it created in his body. "That's sweet of you, Jack. But I didn't do anything. You created all of this for yourself. And you deserve a hundred star-studded evenings to celebrate. I'm just not sure-"

"I need you there, Camille. I need your support." *And so much more.*

"Okay. I see a fancy shopping trip is in my future."

"I can go with you."

A laugh bubbled out of her. "No thanks, buddy. I don't think our styles match."

"Our styles?"

"Well… you like your women a bit more… slutty… than I'm willing to go."

His face fell. "That wasn't very nice, Cam."

"Oh, Jack. Don't be offended. I know exactly who you are.

And I still love you to death. Despite your man-whore ways. Now, what was the date again?"

That first punch landed in his lower stomach, creating a wave of nausea that did not immediately pass.

As JACKSON RODE in the back of the limo by himself, before picking up Camille, he thought about the series of events that had landed him in that particular situation. The words that would end up changing the trajectory of his life had come from her perfect lips.

"You should write a book," she'd said, casually, while they were all cooking dinner together at his Manhattan apartment. But it hit him like a smack in the face. Sure, his academic articles had been getting a lot of attention. And yes, he was a rising star in his profession. But a book seemed out of his league.

With her encouragement, he took on the challenge. He had never worked harder in his life, finishing up his doctorate and writing a book at the same time. It felt like endless nights of toiling away on his computer. And she was there, with bottom-less pots of coffee, pep talks and kicks in the ass, as needed. That's when she transformed in front of his eyes, from the fragile girl with a tragic past, to the powerhouse woman he fell in love with.

The first book was followed by a second book, which caught the attention of a few celebrities. When everything blew up with the third book, he knew exactly what the source of his success had been. And that night he was being honored by an organization he had aspired to for most of his life. Everyone looked to him as a rising star, but there was no question who deserved the credit.

He had decided this was going to be the night he professed his true feelings to her, the night their friendship would become a romance. It was going to be the best night of his life. As he exited the vehicle, Jackson nearly forgot the square box on the seat, and had to turn back to retrieve it. It was a short walk through the courtyard to her apartment. When she opened the door and he got his first look at her, he wished he had taken more time to steady himself. His composure shattered into a million pieces.

"Camille..." There were no words for the sight in front of him.

It was as if she was nude, but everything was covered. The sand-colored dress, which perfectly hugged her curves, allowed for just a peek of her ample cleavage, and only a slice of leg, but there was something so sexy about it that all he could imagine was her naked body. The layers of silk and beading and then something sheer on top created the perfect illusion. It was hard to tell exactly what he was looking at, but it stunned him none-theless.

"Doesn't she look amazing?"

He hadn't even realized that his sister was standing right next to her. "Cam, you are breathtaking."

The top of her chest flushed. "Thanks, Jack. You look great. That suit..."

Even while he gave his sister a quick hug, he couldn't pull his eyes away from Camille.

"Okay, well, I guess I'll be going then." Jenna's voice pulled them both away from the shared gaze. "You guys have an awesome time. I'll be checking for photos online." She gave Camille air kisses on both cheeks, then another hug for him.

"Knock 'em dead, Jack. And you know what I mean." Her whisper into his ear reminded him how much his sister knew about his feelings for Camille. It had been impossible to hide anything from her.

"Actually, we can all head out together." Camille picked up her purse and a shawl from the couch.

"No." His tone was sharper than he intended. "In a minute."

She looked at him curiously. "Sure."

When Jenna closed the door behind her, Camille spoke. "Do you want a drink or something?"

"No. I have something for you. I wanted you to have it before we go."

Camille opened her bright eyes wide.

The black box filled the entirety of his large palm, and he held it out to her. "It's a thank you. For everything you've done for me, for how pivotal you've been in my life, for tonight."

"Oh, Jack. You didn't have to get me anything. It's you we're celebrating tonight. I was going to wait until later, but since you started…" She turned back and picked up a small, dark bag from the kitchen table.

"Cam! No way…"

"Open yours first." She was doing her happy bounce, which nearly dissolved him. The sight of the extraordinarily elegant woman, vibrating like an excited child, warmed everything under his fitted suit.

"If you insist." He put down her box, took the bag from her outstretched hand and pulled out a box that looked very similar to the one he had brought. He was certain it could not contain the same thing. He pulled the large lid open to reveal a watch. His heart beat faster as he recognized every detail. So many years ago, while their dreams were still unformed, he had told her that when he became successful, he would buy himself that watch. She had remembered.

She was beaming when he finally lifted his head to look at her. "Do you like it?"

"Cam, this is way over the top. I can't believe you bought me the Calatrava. I can't accept this." He knew exactly how much the watch cost, and even though she was an heiress, she should not have been spending that kind of money on him.

She lowered her brows. "Don't you dare Jackson King. Don't you dare."

"I don't know what to say."

"I'm so damn proud of you. I just wanted you to know that."

He rolled it off the velvet cuff, snapped open the clasp and slid it onto his left wrist. Wow.

She walked over to examine his arm. "It looks great on you. As I expected."

"Now, you open mine." He picked up the square box and put it in her hand.

He knew she was trying to hide her excitement. That girl loved gifts more than anyone he had ever met. And he loved giving them to her.

Nothing on her face moved as she looked down into the box. He panicked that something had gone wrong, the piece had fallen out, or slipped underneath...

"Holy shit, Jackson." He could see her breath speed up by the movement of her chest. "What..."

Perhaps she was confused about what it was, so he walked over to her side. "It's a bracelet. It screamed your name in the store."

He tried to catch her eyes, but they stayed focused on the jewelry. The wide band of criss-crossing strands of diamonds reminded him of a piece of lace. He had intended to buy a pair of diamond earrings, but as soon as he saw the bracelet, he knew it was the one for her. Other than her inscrutable paralysis, he was certain he had made the right choice.

"Here, let me put it on for you." Still no reaction from her as he slid it off the semi-circular mount and laid it on top of her left wrist. "Cam? You haven't said anything."

She swallowed, then looked up at him. "Jackson, this bracelet... I don't understand. This is *your* night."

"No, love. This is *our* night. Now, let me clasp it for you." His fingers were too big to handle the delicate closures, but she waited patiently for him to find and latch each of the four hooks.

He had been right. It hugged her wrist as if it had been

designed for her. And the weave of the strands was similar to the pattern of her dress.

"Look at us!" He put his left wrist next to hers to compare their new acquisitions. She dropped her arm.

"Cam, what's wrong?"

"I'm just stunned, Jack. I mean, this bracelet is…"

"A small token of my… appreciation." Her words thrown back at her. "You're my secret sauce, Cam. I just want you to know that I realize it."

She wrapped her arms around him. "I love you, Jackson."

"I love you, Camille." *You have no idea how much.*

As SOON AS Camille stepped out of the limousine, she silently thanked Jenna for forcing her to do a couple of dry runs with the dress and shoes. Jenna had grown up a debutante and had ample experience with being graceful in any situation. Camille had not. Her shoes were as impractical as they were beautiful, and her dress was cut to her body with not an inch of give. Walking, sitting, and exiting the car each required their own set of pivots, adjustments, and carefully calculated maneuvers.

She had also mentally prepared to be scrutinized by photographers and media, as well as being completely ignored while they bombarded her now famous best friend. Either way was going to be fine.

The feathery feel of the bracelet on her arm caught her attention every few seconds. She still could not understand why he would buy her such a gift. It was the most beautiful thing she had ever received, but it did not feel deserved.

SHE SQUEEZED his arm with each celebrity sighting, which made him fall in love with her even more. It was that juxtaposition of confident assuredness and fearless vulnerability that catapulted her well above anyone else in his life. She was the only one he could say anything to, without fear of judgment or reprisal. She knew all of his secrets except for one: his feelings for her.

It was painful anytime he had to look away from her, or engage someone else in conversation. But he had to. He worried he was being too obvious. Having her grow suspicious, before they could have a chance to talk about it privately, would ruin the whole plan. Coming clean was going to require every bit of tact and precision he could muster.

"You can just go ask her out, you know," Camille whispered into his ear as they swayed on the dance-floor.

He stopped both of their bodies abruptly. "What are you talking about?"

"That leggy blonde over there. You keep staring at her."

No, I'm just trying not to stare at you. "I'm not staring at her, Cam. And I definitely don't want her number."

"Okay then. But if you change your mind, I'm happy to be your wing man. Just let me know."

That punch landed in the center of his chest, making the next few breaths painful and difficult.

CAMILLE TUCKED herself into the side of his body, resting her cheek on his shoulder, for their long ride home. The soft rhythm of her breath indicated she had fallen asleep. He used the time to review his ultimate plan for the evening. They would go back to her apartment and he would kiss her. Then he would sit her down and explain all he had kept hidden from her, finally free of the biggest secret of his life. She woke as the limo slowed in front of her place.

"Oh my gosh, we're here." She covered her mouth for a tiny yawn. "Sorry I fell asleep. Must have been all that champagne."

He rubbed his thumb in the corner of her sleepy eyes. She pressed her cheek into his palm.

"Thank you so much for tonight, Jack. It was more fun than I could have ever imagined. I can't believe I almost didn't come."

"It was a wonderful night." Jackson steadied himself for what he planned would come next.

"I know I was just your decoy date, but I felt like Cinderella."

The back of his jaw tightened like a fist. "What do you mean by that?"

"If you ever need another pretend plus-one, you can count me in."

She gave him a squeeze and a kiss on the cheek before getting out of the car.

The final punch landed in the center of his throat, making it impossible to say even one more thing.

CAMILLE MOVED on auto-pilot during all of her bedtime preparations. The intricate hairdo had to be disassembled, her face had to be cleaned, her teeth brushed, and she had to find her way out of the dress. It was only after the covers had completely encased her that she let go of the holding at the top of her abdomen. It had been with her since he gave her that bracelet.

It was much too easy to fall into Jackson King. He was the perfect man. No one knew that better than she did, having had access to the best of him for years. When she saw his extravagant gift, the fantastical idea of a love story with him pulled her into hope and surrender. Thank goodness he showed himself during the gala by ogling every beautiful woman around him. And there were plenty to look at. Camille caught him staring away from her a hundred times and she needed that reality check. She was not his and he was not hers. At least not in that way.

Even with all of this crystal clear in Camille's mind, it caused an ache so profound that she cried herself to sleep.

CHAPTER 8

"You better focus, twinkle toes. The Senator is not going to enjoy your stepping on his very important feet."

Camille slumped in Jackson's arms. "Ughhh. Is anyone really going to care?"

"Yes, fry. People care about things like this."

Camille's relationship with a Senator's son, whom she had met in a philosophy class senior year, had progressed enough that she had been invited to a state function. It was black tie, there would be dignitaries from around the world, and she would be expected to dance. Too embarrassed to tell her date that she didn't know how to waltz or foxtrot, she was forced to beg Jackson for dance lessons. Of course, he obliged. Without even one disparaging comment about being a twenty-one year old woman with enormous gaps in her social education.

Her date was almost certainly not going to be as good or exacting a dancer as the man leading her around the room, but it didn't matter. Spending the afternoon in Jackson's arms was not a chore.

"You're doing great, fry. Now, try to pretend you're having fun, okay? Relax your body, smile."

"Right." Another thing to remember.

He whisked her around for a dramatic spin, catching her as she nearly fell into one of his sculptures. Camille held on tight while overcome with giggles.

He righted both their bodies and led her across his living room, in perfect time to the music. "Listen, Cam, there's one more thing. Have you ever had a man tell you he loves you?"

"Jackson!" That one nearly did knock her off her feet.

He tightened his grip around her waist. "This might be your night, fry. I mean you two have been together for a while and it's going to be a romantic evening. You might want to be prepared."

The last man to say those three words to her had been her father, so many years before. "And how does one prepare for such a thing?"

Jackson stopped moving, looked deeply into her eyes, a small smile lifting the corners of his lips. "I love you, Camille."

He had been right, as usual, because nothing in her two decades of life had adequately prepared her to hear those words from that man. Unable to feign composure, or fabricate a response, Camille could only tell the truth.

"I love you too, Jackson."

∽

Now

"What are we doing next, Jackson?" Camille had tried to be as patient as possible, letting him keep the specifics of their dates a secret, but she hated it. The whole thing was creating more than enough tension and anticipation. She was ready for their next step.

He smiled with a twinkle in his eyes. "Pack a bag. We're going away for the weekend."

As soon as they crossed the Golden Gate Bridge, she knew they were headed to Sonoma County. The quieter and more exclusive of the local wine regions was one of their favorite places on the planet. The car pulled into the famed resort Auberge du Soleil and he walked her into one of the two private chalets on the property. Camille's only issue was that they'd only have one night. This setting was her version of paradise.

After putting her few items away, she stood by the enormous windows, looking out at the rolling hillsides covered in the parallel lines of grapevines.

He slipped himself behind her and nuzzled her neck. "Come on, fry. Stop daydreaming. We've got wine to taste."

"First of all, you can't call me fry anymore. We're not those people. Second of all, I'm ready when you are."

He stepped in front of her and cupped the side of her jaw. "You'll always be my French fry. Even when we're old and gray and babysitting our grandkids."

Several quick blinks brought her back after his statement stopped her heart. She reached up to kiss him, lingering long enough to transform her nerves to sweet comfort. After ten years of building a relationship, Camille couldn't have predicted how far they would progress in just two weeks. Her mind and heart had caught up with her body. Resistance and worry had become unshakable love. She was ready.

"Okay, Jack. Let's go. All that Pinot isn't going to drink itself."

SPENDING the day visiting their favorite wineries and strolling the small town could not have been better. The sumptuous meal in the area's most romantic restaurant was the perfect complement. It lived up to every single expectation she had about being with Jackson. All those fantasies, over all those years, looked like the day they'd just had. It wasn't news that he knew how to treat a woman. But he especially knew how to treat her.

There was only one thing missing.

They arrived back at their hotel, tired after a perfectly full day. She wanted to wait for Jackson to undress, but he was taking too long. He moved around the room, as if he was looking for something. She watched and fidgeted.

"Everything alright, Cam?"

"Yes. Fine. I'm... um... going to the bathroom. You get ready for bed. I'll be right out."

When she exited the bathroom, she was hoping that he would notice, but his eyes were closed. As she waited for him, the plan began to sound more and more ludicrous. Maybe this was a huge mistake. Maybe he was right about them not consummating their relationship just yet. Maybe she was making a huge fool of herself.

Just as the idea to duck back into the bathroom and change crossed her mind, his eyes fluttered open.

He blinked as if he couldn't believe what he was seeing. He sat up in bed, face frozen.

Her sheer negligee, in the lightest pink, hadn't been a bad idea, after all. She walked slowly toward him, watching his eyes scan her breasts, the curve of her stomach, the line of her legs, and the small line of hair on her mound. She was clothed, but nothing was actually concealed from view.

"Cam... for me?" She picked up how hard it was for him to form a thought, much less an intelligible sentence.

She knelt astride him and took his face in her hands. "Yes. All for you."

He kissed her so softly, she wondered if he thought she would break. When she offered him her tongue, the energy of his body shifted from shock to hunger. Any tentativeness disappeared.

"You really did this for me?"

"Who else would I do this for? I'm yours. Completely." She knew he was waiting for her to say that, to feel that. There was no question in her mind that becoming her best friend's lover was the right decision.

He slid his hands up the sides of her waist and under her breasts, which were already aching for him. The pull from his mouth and the twist of his fingers created a jolt through her body. She ground herself into him while he nuzzled her breasts. His hands wrapped around to grip her bottom and she rocked forward to press herself farther into him.

"This is so beautiful," he said, fingering the delicate fabric, "but I don't want anything between us."

He pulled the camisole over her head and in a single motion, shifted both of their bodies and put her on her back.

Staying upright, he drew his fingers from her lips down her chin, throat, over her breasts, belly, down the outside of her hip and thigh, and finally back up between her legs. The sensation of just his fingertips hovering over her needy flesh was excruciating. She tilted and arched for him, trying to get more. He slowed down even further.

"You're torturing me."

"Hmmmm…" He dipped his head down and buried it just below her navel, while his fingers slipped between her wet folds and stroked from top to bottom. As he pressed a finger inside her, the tip of his tongue slid along her slit. Her legs fell open and she grabbed handfuls of his hair. He continued to move his finger slowly, and used only the tip of his tongue to discover her.

Camille willed herself to relax.

"Better, love. Better." He rewarded her by increasing the thrust of his finger, and pressing his lips onto her clit. "You taste like heaven."

He sucked in and she yelped. He licked her with the full width of his tongue and she groaned. He focused the tip of his tongue on her clit and her thighs began to quiver.

She pulled at his hair, losing control, as he never let up on the pressure. When he moaned into her, vibrating the entire lower half of her body, she tumbled into an orgasm that radiated from his mouth in every direction. He did not move until she had been still for several breaths, and then brought himself back up her body with an uninterrupted line of kisses. When he hovered above her, Camille's attention was split between his erection pressing against her, and the look on his face.

"You're going to do that a lot for me. When I can watch as well."

She tasted herself when he brought his mouth to hers. "Yes, thank you. Ready when you are."

"Oh really? Does now work for you?" The head of his cock pressed against her opening.

Camille clutched his face to steady herself. She was grateful they'd already had the contraception talk as it took all her energy not to drown in the surreal moment.

She straddled the line between pleasure and pain as he filled her, inch by inch.

"Don't tighten, Cam. Relax, love."

His voice calmed her and she unclenched around him. He brought his head down and she buried herself into his shoulder as he plunged into her. Within a few seconds, they had created a rhythmic dance of pleasure. With a slip of his palm underneath her and a lengthening of his stroke, the tension rose again, crashing into her with another orgasm.

He continued pushing into her, his face strained with emotion and pleasure. She bit into his shoulder and dug her nails into his ass. His breath became panting became groaning became a gravel-filled exclamation. Filled as much as she had ever been by anyone before him, she received each of the pulses into her body.

The last thing she remembered before falling asleep was the look of perfect contentment on his face, and the feeling of utter satisfaction in her body.

· · ·

WITH HER EYES STILL CLOSED, she reached her arm across the bed. Nothing but sheets. A flutter of her eyes brought the bright white empty bed into view. The sound of running water made it clear where Jackson had disappeared to.

Camille stepped into the large shower behind him and pressed her body against his. He spun around to catch her mouth. That quickly, she yearned for the feeling of him inside her again. She broke free of the kiss and turned herself toward the old-fashioned tile wall. All it took was stepping her legs slightly apart for him to find her. His slick body slid against her as his cock plunged inside. Her gasp echoed against the tiles, and then mingled with his own. His palm pressed hers into the wall while his other hand guided her hips back toward him. Any gentleness or tentativeness from the previous night was gone in this fast and furious reclamation.

"Now, Camille. Now."

She responded to his command without hesitation and an orgasm burst through the center of her body. The pulses had not yet stilled when his began, bringing her up and over again.

CAMILLE HAD ALWAYS LOVED the drive from the wine country just north of San Francisco, through Golden Gate Park, and onto the curving roads of picturesque neighborhoods. It contained elements of everything she loved about this part of the world: fields, mountains, curving roads, and the beautiful ocean.

As she was enjoying the sights, Jackson's hand slipped under her skirt, up the inside of her thigh and gently cupped her. "How are you feeling down there?"

"Tender. Sensitive. I can still feel your mouth, your fingers, your cock."

He exhaled audibly. "I was worried that this morning might have been a bit too rough."

"It was great. I loved it."

He squeezed her, which drew a soft groan from her open mouth.

"Damn, fry. I hope you're not too sore."

She considered the question. "Just enough to keep the memories vivid."

He turned to look at her with hunger in his eyes. "I knew you weren't going to be a shrinking violet in bed, but I had no idea…"

The movement of his fingers raised her temperature with each passing second. "What do you mean?"

"When you stepped out of the bathroom, wearing - I don't even know what it's called - that was one of the pinnacle moments of my life."

Camille tipped her head back onto the headrest and allowed a broad smile to fill her face. "Why?"

"Well, first of all, your body is perfection."

The corners of her lips dropped as she imagined the multitude of perfect female bodies he had seen. She had seen some of them too when they were living together. "I've only ever seen you with supermodels. Or women who look like supermodels. I don't look anything like that, Jackson."

"Camille, they are like celery sticks, and you are the juiciest, most perfectly tender steak."

That metaphor made her uneasy. "Any other reason?"

"You radiated power and desire. All the conflict, uncertainty, and worry were gone. The fact that you had been able to do that, in just one week, and that you could come to me with an offer that was so clear and bold, was the sexiest thing I've ever experienced."

"I think you can take credit for at least some of that. Your idea to sleep together naked, crazy as it was, did the trick for me."

"I'm not taking any credit. It was all you. Even your willingness to go along with it demonstrated how remarkable and fearless you are."

"I -"

"I want to go back to your body. You brushed my comment aside."

"Your metaphor made me uncomfortable. It felt cannibalistic."

A throaty laugh came out of him. "You know I don't like games - emotional, verbal, none of it. I don't want you to feel you have to be falsely modest with me. You and I both know that you are a stunningly beautiful woman. Your body is what most guys dream about and few will ever see in person."

She steadied herself. "I appreciate the compliment. I'm just saying that, objectively, I am very different than the women I'm used to seeing you with."

"It's not a coincidence."

She let the weight of that statement drop onto her. Had he been purposely picking women who *weren't* her?

"Fragility is not a turn-on for me. With you, I feel like I can take it as far as I want, without fear of breaking you. And you are emotionally strong enough to define the terms and hold boundaries. Although I hope there aren't that many."

She studied the strong line of his jaw, the outline of his full lips. She wanted everything this man wanted to give her. "Unleash whatever is in there, Jackson. I love the power you hold beneath the surface."

He gripped the steering wheel, whitening his knuckles. "I'm having trouble driving. I want to look in your eyes, and my dick is straining against my pants."

"Pull over."

Without any more discussion, Jackson turned into the large parking lot of a bank, which, because it was Sunday, was nearly empty.

"Push your seat all the way back." Ordering him like this was intoxicating.

She brought herself on top of him, knees straddling his thighs. He slipped his thumb inside the seam of her thong. "You are so fucking wet, Cam."

"For you."

When he slipped his finger inside her, she couldn't help clenching around him.

"I want to feel you do that to my dick."

She lifted off of him enough to maneuver his erection through the opening of his underwear and the zipper of his jeans. While he continued to stroke and dip into her with his finger, she took his rock hard cock into her hand, barely able to close around it. So much she still wanted to explore with him, but for that moment, she needed him inside her.

He pulled at the delicate lace of her underwear. "I'm going to rip these off."

"Yes."

The band tightened against her and then snapped. He buried his face in her breasts as she lowered herself down onto him. Every sensation was heightened on her tender parts.

"Take what you need, Camille. It's all for you."

With a ferocity that matched his from that morning, she rode him, pumping and grinding. When he pinched her nipple, she cried out. When he owned her mouth, she moaned into his. She pulled away to catch her breath, and he bit into the top of her breast, plunging her into waves of orgasm. She called out his name, and he turned up to look at her. Her fingers clenched around his hair while she pulsed around him.

She slowed down only enough to regain her focus. By his expression and his breath, she knew he was close. He grabbed big handfuls of her ass, and pressed himself as deeply inside her as he would go. Keeping her hips pinned, he rocked back and forth, rubbing her against him, and pulling her under again. She squeezed her thighs against him, unprepared for another orgasm. A surge of heat deep inside her and a shattering pulse accompanied the groans that vibrated his whole body.

She dropped herself onto him, as they breathed together. His hands held her body firmly against him.

When she pulled away, his eyes were closed.

"I love you, Jackson."

He raised his eyelids slowly. "I love you, Camille." He moved the hair behind her ear. "I need you to tell me that during a non-intimate moment, okay?"

Was he uncertain of her feelings? "Of course."

He looked down to where they remained connected. "I'm not sure how we're going to deal with this mess, Cam."

She had already started feeling his cum sliding out of her. "I have underwear in my bag, but I think your pants are a lost cause. Do you have an extra pair?"

"I can wear the same pants from yesterday, I guess."

"Your ass looks amazing in those, so it's fine with me."

He raised one eyebrow. "I feel so objectified."

"Get used to it."

TRAFFIC through the city delayed them even further. Camille knew Jackson was worried about showing up to his parent's house late. His father did not tolerate deviance from the rules.

Camille wanted something to take his mind from the minutes ticking by. "We're a pretty unusual couple, don't you think?"

"By design, love. I'm not interested in what's normal or expected or regular. And I love that you've been with me every step of the way. Even when we were just friends, we broke all the rules."

"I'm not sure any platonic friends ever talked about sex as much as we did."

"But look at how well that's worked out." He gave her a wink and a smile.

"Even though you do drive me crazy when you *Dr. King* me, I love how straight and open we are. I mean, for goodness sake, you are the only person who knows all the details of my losing my virginity, and wasn't there."

"I love that about us, too, Cam."

"Did you ever wish it was you?"

He glanced over at her. "Your first time, you mean?"

"Yes."

"Hmmmm... That's a tricky question."

"How so?"

"I wanted it to be wonderful for you, because I cared so much about you. But I don't know that I necessarily wanted to do the deed myself. I know nobody cares about that stuff anymore, but I think it's a big deal. Especially for a woman. It's hard not to get emotionally tangled."

"So, that's a no then?"

"It's not a no. Yes, I was attracted to you. I wanted you. But it wasn't worth the consequence."

"Which was?"

"I don't think we could have created the relationship we did if we had started sleeping together back then. And that's not a price I'd be willing to pay, no matter how delightful your sweet little cherry must have been." He took her hand. "And I much prefer Camille the insatiable sex goddess to Camille the virgin."

CHAPTER 9

ONE YEAR EARLIER

*J*ackson sat on the edge of the bed and checked his watch one more time. This was ridiculous. "Babe, we really have to go."

The gorgeous woman standing in front of the full-length mirror moved her hair from her left shoulder to her right shoulder, followed by a tilt of her head and a pucker.

"Okay, okay." Left. Right. Tilt. Pucker.

"Hon, this isn't a Hollywood party. You can't just show up whenever you want. Please, we need to go."

She turned around with her hands on her tiny waist. "Jackson King, this is an important night. The first time I'm meeting your family and friends. Please don't rush me. I need to look perfect."

"But you always look perfect." That wasn't a lie.

Left. Right. Tilt. Pucker.

He stood up. "Listen, it's going to be very awkward when we walk in there and everyone else is halfway through dinner. Or worse, starving because they've had to wait for us."

She sighed. "Fine."

He followed her ass as she strutted out of the room. It had been in his hands mere moments before. Nothing wrong with that ass, but more exciting in that instant was its movement toward the door.

He drove a bit too fast and a bit too aggressively, but arrived in front of the house with the realization that the last place he wanted to be was inside. He dropped his forehead onto the cool leather of the steering wheel.

"Are you okay, Jackie? Are you having one of your headaches again?"

That word snapped him back up. *Again*. There'd been too many headaches recently. He could rationalize it was all those hours in front of the computer finishing up his latest book. But he knew the truth. The charade had become nearly unbearable. After too many years, he was still having to conceal the biggest lie of his life and his body was rebelling.

"Come on sweetie, let's go inside. You can get some water and take a pain pill."

He turned his head toward the stunning blonde in his passenger seat, giving him that wide-eyed stare that had landed her on stacks of magazine covers. She really was gorgeous.

He stepped out of the car and opened her door. She took his arm and they walked down the garden path to the small, sweet house.

It was time to let go of Camille. Jenna had said this new boyfriend was getting serious. Might even be *the one*. Despite how little he wanted to witness that with his own eyes, it might be the cure he needed. So he could finally let go of the impossible fantasy.

The door swung open as he raised his knuckles to knock. And there she was, beaming at him with the face that was... everything.

"You guys made it!" She jumped into his arms for a quick

hug, then extended her arm. "You must be Katrina. Hi, I'm Camille."

DINNER WAS PERFECT. Jenna and her new guy Edward, Jackson and Katrina, and Camille and Charlie crowded around her slightly-too-small table. But it didn't matter. Camille had cooked a brilliant meal and the house looked beautiful. The only problem was that Jackson's head throbbed all through the meal. He refused to take anything. It was going to be a constant reminder of the ridiculous situation he'd created. And the need for change.

They all convened to the living room after dessert. Jackson was thankful to get up from the table, hopefully far enough away from the others that he didn't have to keep watching Charlie stare at Katrina. That wasn't the only thing that rubbed him the wrong way about that guy, either. Something a little too... entitled... about him. Perhaps the staring was to be expected, though. Katrina's life's work was to make people look at her. And she was very good at it.

Personally, he couldn't take his eyes off Camille. This new level of domesticity was a shock for him to witness. But it seemed to suit her. She looked happy. Despite his early impressions, maybe this was the guy who would do right by her. Maybe they'd get married and live long, happy lives together. He escaped to the kitchen to take a breath, bolts of pain pummeling his forehead. He dropped his head into his palm.

"Hey, Jackson, are you alright? Another one of those headaches?"

The sound of her voice was enough to ease the tension. The fingers on the back of his neck felt like magic.

He lifted his head to give her a grateful smile. "Yeah. It's okay."

She gave him a look that indicated she knew it wasn't. "Want to lay down or something?"

With you. "No." He looked around the room. "Dinner was amazing, fry. Your new nickname might have to be Martha. As in Stewart."

She gave him a playful slap on the arm. "Yes, I know who Martha Stewart is, dummy. And please no more nicknames."

"So, it was nice to finally meet Charlie. He seems like a good guy." What was one more lie?

"Yeah... he's been... great. This whole thing was his idea, actually. He was getting mad that I hadn't introduced him to all the people I kept talking about."

Interesting. "Why do you think that is?"

She squinted at him. "Don't go doctor king-ing me right now. No deep psychological meaning under there. I just wanted to make sure the relationship was stable enough before I brought him in."

"Is it?"

She furrowed her brow.

"Stable enough?" he clarified.

"He's been using the L-word a lot lately. Thankfully, he hasn't been pressuring me to use it."

She hadn't actually answered his question. A smile began to replace Jackson's previously pained expression. "Why is that?"

"Ughhhh, Jackson, can you please stop with the analysis? You know me. I'm not an I-love-you right off the bat kind of girl. It doesn't mean I don't. It just means that I'm not ready to say it."

His smile broke into a wide grin. "That's okay, Cam. Sometimes we can't help who we love. Or who we don't."

She frowned at him. "You're doing that thing I hate. I'm going to bring out another bottle of champagne. Can you try being a little less you while I'm gone?" She laughed as she walked away.

Jackson strutted back out into the gathering with renewed energy, and sat next to Charlie, who was making his way over to Katrina, one inch at a time. Jackson surprised him with a vigorous slap on the back.

"Hey, there, Charlie! What's up, man?"

Charlie coughed and took a moment to wipe the shocked expression off his face. "Nothing much, Jackson. How about you?"

Jackson sat up taller. He was going to win this pissing match. "Oh, just happy to be here with all my favorite people. And glad I finally got to meet you. We were starting to think Cam had made you up."

The shift in Charlie's body language signaled that the challenge had been accepted. "Oh, no worries. I'm definitely real. But Cammy and I have been really busy. Together."

"Good to hear. Good to hear. So, what keeps you busy? What do you do?"

Charlie leaned back into the couch. "I run my family's jewelry business. We're headquartered here, but we've got stores all over the world."

"Wow, man. That's awesome. And we know diamonds are a girl's best friend." He winked, which left the other man with an odd frown.

"And you, Jackson? What do you do?"

"Oh, I-"

"Are you kidding? You don't know who Jackson King is?"

Everyone turned to Katrina, who had momentarily paused her preening to voice her indignation.

Jackson patted her knee. "It's okay, baby. I just wrote a few books. They're not for everybody."

Charlie sat forward in his seat again. His relaxed demeanor had vanished.

"Oh, yeah? Books? What kind of books?"

Jackson waved his hand. "Super boring. Nothing you'd be interested in. I'd love to know more about the jewelry business, though." He slid the sleeve of his shirt above his left wrist. "Check this out, man."

Charlie's eyes popped open as he recognized the rare watch. "Wow, that's quite a timepiece."

"I know, right? Best gift I've ever gotten. From Camille, of course." Jackson took a sip of his drink and relaxed back into his seat. Match - won.

"Jackson!" Jenna popped up out of her seat. "Can you give me a hand in the kitchen? I need to reach... something... on a shelf."

He gave Charlie a pat on the shoulder, much more gently than the first time, as he stood up and followed his sister into the kitchen.

They proceeded past Camille, who was leaning against the sink, and out the back door onto the small patio. Jackson didn't like the look on Cam's face, but didn't have time to investigate while following his sister's brisk pace.

"What the fuck are you up to? What you're doing in there is nine layers of uncool. Do you hear me, Jackson?"

"Whoa, calm down, Jen. What are you talking about?"

She sighed in exasperation. "Don't be an asshole. You're trying to intimidate Charlie. It's obvious to everyone in that room. As if you had some kind of claim over Cammy. Until you grow a set, dear brother, that's never going to happen."

There were few people on the planet that Jackson loved more than his baby sister. But at that moment all her sweet, golden goodness was lost on him. He saw red.

"How dare y-"

"Nope. You're not going to do your psychobabble manipulation. You have no leg to stand on here. Or have you forgotten that you are at this party with your bimbo-du-jour? What? Are you going to ask Katrina to step away while you profess your undying love to Camille? Is that your master plan?"

It felt as if someone was inserting a railroad spike between his eyes. He reached out to a table to catch his balance.

"Jack! What's going on? Are you alright?"

He slowed his breathing and focused on the slate pavers. He

looked up at his sister when the intensity diminished. "I don't want to fight with you, Jenna. I'm not sure why you're so heated up about this - it has nothing to do with you - but I want you to know that I've heard your concerns."

"Fuck you, Jackson. Don't dismiss this."

He slammed his hand down on the table. "What, exactly, do you want me to do? Hmmm? You're the only person in that room who knows what's going on. So would you please, just give me a goddamn break?"

The rage that had brought a flush to her cheeks began to pass. "I'm not trying to attack you, Jackson. I'm just frustrated. With both of you. It should just be easy."

"I'm not sure things like this are ever easy, sweetheart."

"Attacking her new boyfriend is not the way to her heart. Doctor Jackson King is much smarter than that." She touched his temple. "Sorry you're not feeling well. Can I do anything?"

"No. I have to take care of this situation myself."

Jenna wrapped herself around her big brother. He kissed the top of her head, with a growing gratitude for the reality check she'd just given him. The back door swung open, startling both of them out of their lingering hug.

"Hey, you guys! What's going on out here? Party's still going on inside."

Camille's words floated over him as he watched her wipe her hand on her skirt, then tuck a stray hair behind her ear. Her smile brightened the encroaching darkness of the night.

"Sure, fry. We'll be right in. Love you."

"Love you too, Jackson."

His sister put her palm on his chest and shook her head.

Camille stepped back into the living room. Her dinner party had gone terribly wrong. Both Charlie and Edward had given up trying to pretend not to blatantly stare at Katrina, who hardly looked up from her phone. Jenna and Jack were outside doing God knows what. She hoped they weren't fighting, but they both looked upset.

She cleared her throat to confirm her presence in the room. Everyone jumped.

Charlie smiled awkwardly. "Hey, babe. Everything alright?"

"Yes. Sorry I took so long in the kitchen. Anybody need anything?"

No one answered. Large, warm hands wrapped around her waist, causing her own silent shock.

"Why don't we play a game?" said Jackson from behind her, perching his chin on her shoulder.

Eyes opened wide, mouths stayed closed.

Jenna entered the room. "That's a great idea!"

Camille really wanted Jackson to move his hands and body off her. She took a big step forward. "What should we play?"

"How about Truth or Dare?" Charlie finally spoke up, but what came out of his mouth was certainly suboptimal.

Katrina made a face as if she'd smelled something bad. "Isn't that a bit juvenile?"

"Oh, come on, Kat. It'll be fun. And a great way to get to know each other." At Jackson's comment, Katrina batted her voluminous eyelashes and smiled.

Jackson picked up his glass of water from the coffee table. "I think we should do teams. Couples. No actual couples or siblings. Which leaves me with… Camille."

Her eyes flitted between Jackson, who grinned, and Charlie, who glowered.

"I pick Katrina." Edward spoke up.

"I guess it's you and me, Charlie." Even Jenna couldn't muster excitement for that.

"Uh… how do you play Truth or Dare with teams?"

"Good question, Charlie. Let me explain."

Something about the way Jackson spoke to Charlie made Camille's stomach turn. She wished she knew what was going on with him. Did he have something against her new boyfriend? Is that what he and Jenna were arguing about?

It wasn't like Jackson to be so rude. Or passive aggressive. Camille swore under her breath, wondering how her closest friends had turned her lovely dinner party into an awkward collection of pained expressions. "Why don't I get a few more bottles first?"

"I'll help you!" Jenna moved faster than Camille had ever seen and led them both into the kitchen. She went straight to the fridge and pulled out two more bottles of champagne.

"Hey, Jen, what's going on with everyone? Especially Jackson?"

Jenna didn't stop unwrapping the foil covering the cork. "Nothing to worry about, Cam."

"Hmm… Are you guys fighting?"

Jenna spun around to face her friend. "No, hon, we're not fighting. He's just… you know… he's so protective of you. It's new for him to see you this… close… to someone. Please don't worry about it. Your party is perfection. Seriously." She handed Camille a glass of champagne filled to the brim. "Nothing that a bit of bubbly can't fix."

Awkward silence greeted the two women as they returned. Camille swallowed a pervasive sense of defeat.

Jackson accepted his glass from Jenna. "Great. So here's how it works. One partner will choose truth or dare and the other will provide the question or situation. If the truth isn't told, or the dare isn't completed, another couple has the chance to steal, using the same questions asked. So, we've got six rounds. The couple with the most points wins. Got it?"

Katrina opened her mouth, then snapped it shut. She emptied her glass.

Jackson continued. "I think it should be ladies first. Agreed?"

Silence.

"Okay, I'll go first. And I choose dare." Thank God for Jenna. Always game.

Charlie looked at her as if she had grown an additional nose or breast. He stared, unspeaking.

"Hey, Charlie, there's an app that has great Truth or Dare questions if you can't think of any." Jenna tried to encourage him with a forced smile. "Maybe we should all take a look."

Four hands simultaneously reached for four phones. Camille didn't shift her attention from Jackson. "You already know what you're going to ask?"

"I do. And you?"

"I'll wing it."

His laugh brought all the scattered attention back to him. And to them. There wasn't enough champagne to make that feeling of dread go away. This was a bad idea.

Charlie rubbed his hands together. "I'm ready now. I've got a dare for you, Jenna."

She sat forward in her seat. "Go ahead."

"I dare you to kiss Camille. On the mouth."

Jenna's lip curled in the clearest display of disdain Camille had ever seen on her sweet face. She might have even rolled her eyes. "Oh, I see. We're playing *that* kind of game. Okay."

She got up, walked around the coffee table to the middle of the couch, took Camille's face in her hands and kissed her. For much longer than anyone, including Camille, was expecting.

With no hint that anything extraordinary had just happened, Jenna returned to her seat and smiled. "Done. How many points is that?"

Camille heard Charlie swallow from across the room. "Damn," he grunted.

"That's one point for Jenna. Well played, sis." Jackson looked around the room. "Who's next?"

Not that Camille tried, but Katrina easily took the slot.

"It's dare for me." She winked and sent Jackson a kiss.

Edward sat up taller in his seat. "Your dare is... do a lap dance."

Camille groaned, exasperated. "Are we really going to have all the women live out your fantasies?"

Jackson tapped his chin. "Well…"

"Oh, I'm fine with it." Katrina had already stood up. "I just don't know who I'm doing it for."

Jackson beamed. "I think the hostess should continue getting all the attention."

Edward nodded. "Yeah. Great idea, Jackson. For Camille."

The smiles among all three men were completely outmatched by the frown on Camille's face.

"Wait, I'll put some music on." Jackson fiddled with the bluetooth system accessed through his phone until a popular song rang through the house. Katrina did not miss a beat. She strutted over to Camille and undulated her body to the beat. It crossed Camille's mind that it might not have been Katrina's first time.

It wasn't bad at all. In fact, Katrina was pretty remarkable to look at. Physically perfect, as far as Camille could tell. And she could dance. She might have crossed the line just a bit with her grand finale of pushing Camille's face into her impressive breasts, but it did take Camille's mind off the worrying turn of her dinner party. When the song ended, Camille stood up and applauded Katrina with the same vigor as everyone else in the room. In response, Katrina gave a theatrical bow and blew a series of grand kisses.

"Wow. Katrina earned her point. Nicely done." Jackson turned to the last remaining woman in the room. "And you?"

"I choose truth."

He smiled, giving her that look she had long understood to mean he already knew what she was going to say. She shook her head, annoyance mounting and mingling with concern about what devious request he would make of her.

"Tell us, dear Camille, in great detail, an unfulfilled sexual fantasy."

A gasp and some rustling from across the table didn't pull her laser focus from Jackson. Whatever game he was playing, she was going to win. She slowly crossed her legs and pursed her lips. Borrowing from Katrina's playbook, she even flipped her hair.

"Let's see..." She took a generous gulp of champagne. If her heart weren't beating so damn hard, she might have appreciated the dead silence of the room.

"We're in a car. All dressed up, probably. Watching him drive, the muscles of his arms flexing, is turning me on. I run my hand along his thigh and rest it between his legs. I can feel the revving of the engine through his taut body. I squeeze and he hardens beneath my palm. His grip on the steering wheel tightens as he weaves in and out of traffic. We're going fast.

"He takes one of his hands off the wheel and slides it under my skirt. His fingers slip beneath my thong and stroke me. By the time he presses into me, I'm so wet and wound up, I come almost immediately."

Somebody moaned. Camille continued. "He pulls his hand out, puts his fingers in his mouth and sucks. I nearly come again.

"He turns into a parking lot and stops the car. Without saying anything, he slides his seat all the way back and I straddle him. I free his rock hard cock from his pants. He positions my hips and enters me. Right there, in the middle of a parking lot, where anyone can see, we fuck. Like crazy."

Camille took a breath and looked around the room. A series of shocked, flushed faces stared back at her. A satisfied grin escaped from her own face. None of them had to know that the other participant in her fantasy was not, in fact, her boyfriend.

JACKSON AGGRESSIVELY THOUGHT about his grandmother. And

puppies. And golf. Anything to subdue the raging situation in his pants.

"Okay, then. Whose turn is it now?" Camille's voice did not help.

Roadkill. Stock market crashes. Starving children.

"Holy shit, Cam." Jenna fanned herself. "I'm not sure we can go on after that. You might have just closed the game down."

"That's not fair! The guys didn't have to do anything humiliating."

Jackson cleared his throat. "Was that humiliating for any of you?"

The women answered in near unison. "Nope."

"Still not fair," Camille said.

He could not stop staring at her. He could just picture himself in that car with her. He squeezed his eyes shut. "I'll go." It couldn't be any worse than managing what had now become a recognizable ache.

She turned her head so slowly, he almost died with anticipation. "Truth or dare, Jackson?"

"Truth."

"Excellent. Tell me… what scares you the most?"

He hoped she hadn't noticed his involuntary flinch. How could he tell the truth and hide it at the same time?

He looked around the room, eventually catching his sister's eye. She nodded. He could do this.

"I'm afraid that the vision I have for my life won't come true. That everything I've worked so hard to achieve and create will be meaningless because the one, most important thing, will be missing."

He shifted in his seat. "I'm afraid that I might be too late. That what I've been waiting for, planning for, is already out of my reach. I'm terrified I won't know what to do if and when I ever get the chance to…"

Words did not fail Jackson King. Ever. But he couldn't continue, so they all sat in silence.

Had anyone else in the room understood what he was concealing? His sister certainly had. Perhaps Katrina as well? Did he want Camille to know he was talking about her?

Jenna stood up. "It's getting late, everybody. After that inspirational round from my brilliant brother, I think we're going to have to get going. Team Cam-n-Jack take home the championship. Well played, everyone."

Jackson stood up. His sister had saved him. The other men in the room looked bored or confused. He couldn't tell which. Katrina yawned. He refused to look at Camille. It would have been too much.

"I guess we'll head out too."

Jenna picked up an empty bottle and two glasses. "Jackson, help me clean up a minute."

He gathered two handfuls and followed his sister into the kitchen, prepared for another talking-to.

As soon as her hands were free, she wrapped him in a hug. "I love you, Jackson. It's going to be alright."

He relaxed in her arms. "Thanks, bunny. Love you."

She pulled away and chuckled. "You mean you're not mad at me for making out with your girl waaaaay before you?"

"Oh, you'll pay for that."

GOODBYES WERE BRIEF, which was for the best. Jackson's headache had returned and he'd have to figure out how to deal with Katrina. She'd stayed uncharacteristically quiet for most of the night, which only meant one thing. She had an enormous amount to say about someone or something. All he wanted was to get home, close his eyes and replay that scene in the car, over and over again.

CHAPTER 10

NOW

*J*ackson and Camille collected themselves as they pulled into the circular driveway of the King home. He took her hand. "I'm going to tell my family. About us."

She had assumed he would. "Jenna already knows."

"I figured. But I want to tell them all. They love you so much, Camille. I'm sure they're going to be really happy for us."

In theory, this was not a problem. But something in the back of her mind made her wonder if it was too soon to be making their new relationship public. And she prayed he'd be subtle about it.

Sunday gathering at the King house was a longstanding tradition, involving the immediate family, significant others, random guests and visiting dignitaries. No one was excused, not even Camille, who had long ago been inducted as one of the family. That week, however, she would not only be attending as one of the family, but also as Jackson's love interest. She paused with one foot out of the car and grappled with the idea of not going in. This was scary and she didn't like it.

Jackson's love life had frequently been a topic of conversation, primarily because of the celebrities involved. But this time, she'd be the target. Even though she knew this family better than any other, it felt impossible to predict how they would react to the dramatic shift in their relationship and her status.

Jackson and Camille walked in the door to a bustling household. Julian was giving a theatrical rendition of something that happened to a rapt audience of his family. She always had the sense that if he hadn't felt so much pressure from his family, he might have easily gone into theater.

"Hi everybody."

Julian's story was interrupted by the rush for greetings and hugs. Camille was pleased to see that they might have gotten away with their tardy arrival until Mr. King entered the room, scowling and looking at his watch. He clasped his son on the shoulder, and then softened to give Camille a hug.

"I'm so sorry we're late, Mr. King. Jackson warned me that we were going to hit traffic coming back from Sonoma, but I didn't believe him. I delayed our departure and made us late."

She saw the small smile that crept across Jackson's face at her deception.

Jonathan planted a kiss on Camille's head. "That's no problem, Camille. I'm just glad you're here."

At least two people rolled their eyes at Jonathan's soft spot for her.

"You two were in Sonoma?" asked Mrs. King.

"Yes, Mom. I got you a case of the Syrah you love. I forgot it in the car." Jackson headed back out the door.

Mrs. King looked delighted. "Oh, that's so sweet of you." She tilted her head toward Camille. "How was it, dear?"

"Oh, beautiful, as always. We both really love it up there."

"Who doesn't?" Jenna was not being subtle at all in checking her out. "Cammy, come upstairs with me for a minute, will you?"

Without waiting for a response, she whisked Camille up the stairs to her childhood bedroom, which was still decorated as if she were sixteen.

As soon as the door closed, Jenna turned to face her. "Holy fuck!"

"What is it, Jenna?"

"Did you two fuck in the car on the way here? You kind of look like it. And smell like it."

Camille burned with embarrassment. "Are you serious?"

"I'm sure my parents can't tell, if that's what you're worried about."

Camille walked over to the mirror and tried to organize her hair that was admittedly tussled. "Dammit."

"What the hell happened up there?"

Camille bit her lip, trying to hide the enormous smile wanting to erupt out of her face. "Everything happened, Jenna. Everything."

Jenna's already enormous blue eyes widened to half the size of her face. "Oh. My. God. So, it's done. You two are officially fucking?"

Camille huffed. "We're doing more than fucking, Jen."

"Yeah, yeah, right. You're in love, blah, blah, blah."

"Such a romantic you are." Camille grabbed her friend's hands. "I think he's going to tell everybody."

"What do you think he's going to say? Hey everybody, you know how we all consider Camille our sister? Well, she ain't. I know because I'm bangin' her."

"God, Jenna, you are so obscene."

"That's why you love me."

"I can't even talk to you about this if you're going to act like that. I'm going to the bathroom."

Jenna wagged her finger. "Make sure to wash my brother's business off of you while you're in there."

"Ugggghhh!"

ELENA KING, the consummate hostess, prepared a deliciously impressive meal, accompanied by nonstop conversation. The one thing the King family never lacked was opinions and the will to share them. As the meal came to an end, Camille wondered how and when Jackson was going to inform his family of their news. She didn't have to wait long. He stopped his mother from serving dessert to bring a bottle of champagne out of the fridge. After filling all the glasses, he lifted his own. "I'd like to make a toast, everyone."

He was greeted with wide eyes and curious expressions from everyone around the table except for Jenna, with a Cheshire grin, and Camille, horrified. A public announcement was the last thing she wanted.

"Well, I have big news that I want to share with you." He turned down to look at Camille. She wanted to dissolve. "Camille and I have been the best of friends for ten years, as you all know. We realized, recently, that the feelings we have for each other had outgrown our friendship. I've been lucky enough to convince her to give me a chance as a partner, as her love. So, I want to toast the person whom I credit with so much of what is good, the love of my life. To Camille!"

CAMILLE LOOKED around the room to the variety of responses. Justin looked bored, Julian pleasantly surprised, Elena's lower lip trembled, Jonathan thinned his lips, and Jenna held her self-satisfied grin.

"Haven't you two been together forever?" Justin looked up from his phone to share the fact that he couldn't have been less impressed or interested.

"No, Justin, we've just been friends. Until now." Jackson had very little patience for his baby brother.

"That makes no sense." Justin went back to his phone.

Elena walked between the two of them and brought an arm around each of their shoulders. "I could not be happier. You two are perfect together!"

Camille tilted her head up at her boyfriend's mother. "Thank you, Mrs. King."

Elena looked over at her husband. "Isn't it wonderful, Jonathan?"

"It is certainly quite a surprise."

Camille recognized the chill in the elder's voice, and gave Jackson's hand a squeeze knowing his father's response would upset him.

Fatigue hit Camille hard as they gathered in the living room after dinner. She leaned over to whisper in Jackson's ear. "Will you be ready to go soon, honey?"

His face relaxed more than it had the entire evening. "There's nothing better I'd like to do than take you home." He stood and addressed the group. "Well, everyone, we're going to head home now. Thanks for another amazing meal, Mom. Good to see you all." He turned to help Camille up, when his father appeared by her side.

"Actually, before you two take off, I need a minute with Camille." Jonathan took her arm. "It's business stuff. Nothing you'd be concerned with."

Camille reluctantly stood up and let herself be led out of the room, Jonathan's hand at her back.

This was not the first time she had been invited to his office to discuss business, but something about this instance left her highly unsettled.

He sat on the edge of his large cherry wood desk and smiled at her. She fidgeted in the overstuffed leather chair that threatened to swallow her entire body. "What can I do for you, Mr. King?" She wanted to get home. Or at least get out of that room.

He walked around his desk and absently moved some

papers around. "A new tech company prospectus landed on my desk and I thought of you."

"Really? What are they doing?"

"They've got this brilliant algorithm that pulls data from public and private sources. It's a hybrid search engine. Brilliant stuff, really. I'll probably invest, and thought you might be interested in checking them out. I know that big corporate job isn't keeping you engaged."

She regretted once telling him that she was getting frustrated with how slow everything moved at her company. "It's not that bad. I'm learning so much. But I'll take a look at them. Are they looking for help?"

"Not yet. But they will need to. It's just a bunch of kids who have limited vision. They need someone like you who can take them to the next level."

"I really appreciate your confidence in me. It means so much, especially from someone who's achieved all you have."

"You forget, Camille, I've been following you since Princeton. There are great things in your future. You are an amazingly talented girl. I don't want to see you wasting your talents with someone who doesn't appreciate them."

She got the strong sense he was no longer talking about her job.

"Listen, I'm going to speak frankly here."

Camille held her breath.

"I know that you are in a strong financial position. You don't need this job to put food on the table. The only way you're going to make your mark in this industry is to get in on something new and risky. Or to start something yourself. Now, you're just feeding a machine that's already built."

"I understand, sir. And I agree with you. I will look at this company if you think it has potential. I just don't have your perspective and experience to be able to assess all these small operations. I'd hate to pick the wrong one."

"It happens. Even to the best of us."

Camille stood up. "Okay. I look forward to getting your information. And again, I appreciate your looking out for me. It's an honor that you've taken an interest in my career."

"I've taken an interest in everything about you, Camille. You have been more of a daughter to me than my own children."

"I don't know what to say. It's me who thanks you and your family for taking me in when..." This was not the time to get emotional.

She moved toward the door, but he took her arm. "There's one more thing, dear."

A brick dropped in the bottom of her gut. "Yes, sir."

"This thing with you and Jackson..."

Her face began to warm.

"I love my son, and I'm proud of all he has achieved. I'm just not sure..."

Camille sealed her lips shut.

"I'm not sure he's husband material."

Camille could not hold back a gasp. "Sir, we have just begun a relationship. It's not-"

"That's what I mean, Camille. He has created a certain life-style for himself, to my dismay. You deserve better than that. I would hate for my son to do anything that would hurt you."

Camille opened her mouth to speak, but her body shook so badly, she couldn't manage a single word. A thread of terror wrapped itself around her throat. There was nothing good about what Jackson's father had just said to her, whether it was true or not.

"I hope you can take this in the spirit it was given. I really care about you, Camille. I only want the best for you."

"Thank you, sir." Camille brought her hand to the cool brass knob, turned it to open the door and stepped out of the room.

JACKSON TOOK her hand as they drove home. He had not

stopped sneaking looks at her. "What's going on, love? You look upset."

"I'm so tired. That's all."

"What happened with my father?" She could tell he was working to keep his voice calm.

"He's investing in a company he wants me to work for."

"Still with that? He's the only person on the planet who thinks that working at Google isn't good enough."

"He did make a point. I can't deny that I'm in a position that I could take big career risks without the fear of being homeless."

"Because of your inheritance?"

"Yeah."

"But that doesn't mean you should. Not everyone is suited for that. Maybe you're super happy at Google. Maybe you enjoy being part of a globally impacting company, as opposed to working out of some kid's garage."

"Yeah…" Camille's head was spinning so fast, she had no idea what she wanted.

CAMILLE HARDLY SLEPT, so disturbed by Jonathan's statements about his own son. How dare he? She knew better than to bring it up with Jackson until she could do it without emotion. His rage would be bad enough, without her adding to it.

She woke up to find him gazing at her. "You look exhausted, love." He ran his fingers across her brow. "How about I cook you dinner tonight, we eat in our pajamas, and get an early night?"

"That sounds perfect, honey. You always know what I need."

"That's what I'm here for."

When she returned home after work to find her apartment cleaned, and smelling like an Italian restaurant, she almost forgot the burden she had been carrying all day. Jackson greeted her with a deep kiss and an extended hug.

She softened in his arms. "I could get used to this."

"Please do."

"So, you're going to quit that pesky professor job and just be my houseboy?"

"You have no idea how much I'm considering that idea. And we have all summer to actually test it out first, don't we?"

Even though it had been years, Camille consistently forgot that Jackson had the summers off. Unlike most of his peers, who had to teach classes and push brutal publishing schedules, his fame and the resultant attention it gave the university allowed him much more flexibility.

"It looks like you spent the whole day cooking and cleaning." The degree to which he had worked on her apartment became evident as she looked around. No one would ever accuse her of being a neat-nick. And her place almost gleamed.

"No. It didn't take that long. I actually got through all of the edits on the new book. All that great sex has definitely fueled efficiency in me."

"Glad to help."

He brought two glasses of red wine from the kitchen. "Unless you're starving, let's sit down for a minute. I have a couple of things I want to run by you."

As do I. "I'm going to change, okay?"

"Can I watch?"

"Do I have a choice?"

"Good point." He followed her into the bedroom.

It felt so good to kick off her shoes and peel the layers off. Her work environment was casual, but she had decided to always dress professionally. It was hard enough to be taken seriously as a young, attractive woman. She wanted everyone to understand she was very serious about her job.

He watched her get undressed with a sweet smile on his face. "How was work, love?"

"Fine. Normal Monday. Your Dad sent me his analysis on that new company, so I spent some time going over it. I have to say their technology was very impressive. I might consider working with them."

"Really?" He did not look altogether pleased.

"We'll see."

"Are you ever going to tell me what really happened with my father?"

Camille slipped on her favorite sleep shirt, unconcerned with its complete lack of sexiness. "You're not going to like it."

"I figured."

"You didn't press me on it last night. I appreciate that."

"I know you, Camille. I'm not always going to get it right, but I hope I can more often than not make choices that honor how you want to be treated."

She wrapped her arms around his neck, standing on her toes to be face to face. "Have I told you how much I love you?"

"Not recently."

"Have I shown you how much I love you?"

His eyes widened. "Cam…"

Her hands moved swiftly to the button of his jeans, then the zipper, then his black boxers. He pulled his t-shirt off, then helped her with the shirt she had just put on. She pushed him back on the bed, crawled up to meet him, and put his already stiff cock deep into her mouth.

"Aaaaah…" he growled.

There was nothing delicate or demure about how she owned the whole of him, sucking, licking and tonguing every part of him. She cupped his balls, pressed the area just behind them, and gripped him as if she was holding on for balance. She did not pause or slow her relentless pace until he erupted into the back of her throat.

Camille dropped her head on his stomach, panting from the exertion.

"Holy fuck, Camille. Please tell me you haven't always been able to do that."

She lifted her head. "What?"

"Come up here." He hooked under her shoulders and pulled her up to him. "I might have to change my previous statement about it being a good thing that we waited, if this is something you were capable of back then."

"Don't be silly, Jackson. That's the first blowjob I've ever given."

He gave her bottom a smack that sounded throughout the room. "I'm going to ignore the sarcasm and tell you that that was amazing. But perhaps you already knew that."

She twirled her fingers around the small collection of hairs in the center of his chest, snuggled her head into his shoulder and closed her eyes.

When she opened them again, he was hovered on top of her. She bent her knees to open herself more for him, and shifted her hips to position him at her opening.

He entered her slowly in small pulses while her body relaxed enough to take him in. She loved the feeling of tightness, the stretching, the pressure of him finding his way inside her.

She looked up at him, a man in complete control of himself and his environment. There was no sign she could give that he wouldn't record and utilize, possibly no emotion she would feel that he wouldn't recognize and respond to. She closed her eyes, unable to focus in the swarm of delights. He was gentle with her, knowing that she was probably still tender, and perhaps knowing that it was perfect for her body and her emotional state.

When her breathing accelerated and her groans deepened, he lengthened the strokes. Staying up on one hand, he slipped the other underneath her bottom and brought himself even deeper. This tipped her into the rolling waves of the most buttery orgasm she had ever felt, free of fever and spikes, all languorous slow release.

She opened her eyes to find him exploring her face with his eyes, full of wonder and awe. "Oh, Camille. I cannot handle how beautiful you are." He kissed her with a delicateness unexpected after what they just shared.

When he pulled out of her and lay to one side, she curled into his body. She was wide awake.

"Tell me about my father."

"Jackson, I don't want to ruin this moment. Why don't you tell me your news."

"I'm thinking of taking a sabbatical."

She inhaled sharply. "Jackson!"

"The idea's been bouncing around for a while. The next book is nearly done, there'll be a book tour, media, all that. And I've already got an idea for the next book."

"But you've always done that while still keeping your position."

"I know, but I've been wondering if I really need to. If I could just write, do some speaking and lecturing, that would be perfect. And frankly, I want to create space in my life for you."

A tickle of fear lodged itself at the base of her throat. She waited for it to pass. "Jack, I would never second guess your perspective. You've built a remarkable career from nothing. I just don't want you to make these huge life decisions based on the last week of your life."

He turned to face her. "There's something about that that bothers me, Cam. Are you telling me to wait and see how it goes with us?"

Sometimes it was hard to have a conversation with someone who was so damn literal. "Yes, that's what I'm saying. But it's not because I have doubts about us, it's just we don't know how it's going to look. How we're going to split our time and-"

"What did my father say to you, Camille?"

Fuck. There was no use hiding it anymore. "Please don't think it has any relevance. I know you're going to draw a thread between the events that just isn't there."

"Spill it."

She swallowed. "Mostly, he talked about wanting me to take more risk with my career. Go work for a startup."

"And?"

"He said that he wasn't sure you were husband material, and that your past behavior might make you an unsuitable match for me." She wanted to be sick.

His expression did not change one millimeter, which was the scariest thing she had ever seen. Abruptly, he got up and walked out of the bedroom. She followed him, watching as he took his phone off the kitchen counter, clicked a few buttons and put it up to his ear.

"Dad? Hi, it's Jackson. Fine, thanks."

His voice was like a blade. "I just wanted to let you know that I know what you said to Camille. I understand that there's something about me that has always rubbed you the wrong way, but to sabotage the best thing that has ever happened to me has crossed a line I can't come back from. Please consider this goodbye. I will no longer be part of your life."

With an eery calmness, he put the phone back down on the granite counter and turned to Camille. "Ready for dinner?"

CHAPTER 11

*C*amille recoiled at the look on Jackson's face. Icy calm was his highest expression of rage, something she'd seen only once or twice in their ten years of friendship. He'd just hung up the call with his father and hadn't addressed her confession at all. What his father had said was inexcusable. But was she going to be blamed for it?

"Jackson, please come back in here. Let's talk about this."

"Not right now, honey. I'm starving. You must be too."

He moved efficiently through the kitchen, gathering plates, utensils, and platters. He set the table, put all the food out, and sat down while she stood frozen in the bedroom doorway, growing more and more concerned.

"Come, sit down, Cam. The food's getting cold."

She grabbed a robe from the back of the door and did as she was told. "Jackson…"

"Oh, I forgot to tell you. The other reason for the sabbatical is that the next book is going to require a ton of research. I'm looking at the mindset of longevity in intimate relationships. And I was hoping you would help me with it."

Camille struggled to hold back the tears burning across her

temples. He would never have stated this so casually if he was in his right mind.

He continued. "But now, I think it's probably best if I just quit outright. I mean, I really only got that job to impress my father, so he could say, 'My son teaches at Stanford', instead of being constantly embarrassed that I only write pop psychology books with no intellectual value."

She reached out and touched her fingertips to his forearm. He looked down at her hand, as if it had appeared from a different planet. Then she noticed the quake in his shoulders and the cloudiness in his eyes. Camille pushed out of her chair and pulled his head into her body. The move released the last of the hold he had, and he exploded into her, shaking and sobbing. She stroked his hair, whispered to him, and held on.

They went straight to bed after dinner, even though it was barely 9pm. He laid his head on her chest.

Her heart broke for him. "Jackson, you've always been the strongest person I know. I want to help you through this, but I just don't know what to do. I'm sorry. I wish I could be better at this."

"Cam, there's nothing you need to do. This isn't your problem."

She shifted his head to catch his eye. "Please don't say that. Of course it's my problem. Because something is hurting you. And I want to help."

"I don't want to talk about it anymore, okay? Goodnight, love."

She wondered when they were going to talk about it at all.

JONATHAN KING WAS a bit of a legend in Silicon Valley. First as one of the hi-tech originals, then as a brilliant investor and the man behind many of the newest generation of success stories. He had the magic touch in technology. When he walked through the maze of one of the programming floors at Google, whispers followed him like a celebrity sighting. He appeared at Camille's door, just as his son had several years before. What was with these King men, thinking that they could just show up at her place of work?

"Mr. King."

He placed his hands on the back of the chair meant for visitors. And for sitting. "We have a problem, Camille."

"I know. I'm sorry about what happened. It just wasn't right for me to keep a secret from Jackson-"

"It's fine. I should have known. Now, the only question is, how are we going to fix it?"

Her eyes narrowed. "We?"

His attention moved to the mess on her desk. "Clearly, I need your help to make a case with my son. He refuses to communicate. It's been days. I'm sure you can talk some sense into him."

Camille tried to inconspicuously bring the scattered papers into a neat stack. "I appreciate you coming all the way down here, but there's no way I can get in the middle. This is between you and your son, and anything I might do would look like taking sides. I really don't want to do that."

He took one step back. "I'm disappointed by that, Camille."

She steeled herself for some further elaboration or a repeat of the request. Instead, he stood silent.

Camille watched one of the assistants approach the office, stop abruptly, and turn around. There was no winning a stand-off against Jonathan King, who was nearly as hard to refuse as his son. "Alright. Let me talk to him and see what can be done."

"That sounds fine. Thank you." His expression snapped from steely to smiling.

"Mr. King?"

"Yes, dear." Even the tone of his voice softened. This was how she was used to him - kind, caring, even a tiny bit sweet.

"I suggest being honest with Jackson. For whatever reason,

he's felt rejected by you his whole life. I think this was his last straw. Perhaps figuring out why he had that idea, and how you can convince him otherwise, would be a good start."

He nodded. "I'll keep that in mind."

Jonathan patted the back of the chair before walking out of the office. Camille fell back into her chair, heart pounding, wondering how her life had all of a sudden become theatrical.

CAMILLE WAITED two days to bring up the issue. She hoped Jackson would have changed his mind and offered to talk about it. He never did.

She approached him at his desk in the spare room furiously typing on his computer. She put her hands on his shoulders. "Your dad came to see me. A couple days ago."

He didn't stop typing. "Yes. He's been sending me messages. Wants to talk." He looked up at her. "I'm disappointed it took you this long to tell me. I didn't realize we were keeping secrets."

Now everyone was disappointed.

Camille shook her head. "I waited because I thought time would provide some perspective. You can't just pretend nothing is happening. And it's going to be very difficult to avoid your father for the rest of your life."

"I do difficult things all the time." The gravel of his voice was full of rage and spite.

She took her hands off him and stepped back. "Are you angry with me?"

He turned to face her. "I'm frustrated. I've told you I don't want to discuss this with you, and I certainly don't want you involved, but you keep pushing it."

Her heart pounded in her ears. "Why don't you want me involved?"

"You and my Dad have some weird thing. I don't know if he

wants you or pities you or something else. But clearly you don't see straight about each other."

The last threads of her compassion and control burst into flames. "You have no right, Jackson. You have no fucking right!"

She stormed into the bedroom to gather her things, her entire body pulsing with rage. That was the single cruelest thing he had ever said to her. She could hardly recognize the man she thought she knew so well. It wasn't even clear whose clothes she was shoving into her bag. She just needed to get out of there.

He stopped her as she headed toward the door. "I'm sorry, Cam. What I said was crass. Don't rush out of here like this."

"Are you not quite done lashing out at me? Because I'm done."

Panic filled his expression as he gripped her arms tightly. "Cam. Don't do this. You know I'm heading out of town tomorrow, and I don't want to leave it like this. I apologize for what I said. Now let's move on."

She pushed his hands off her. "Goodbye, Jackson. Have fun in LA." She did not even close the door behind her, just kept walking.

IT WAS a relief to bury herself in work while Jackson was out of town. She had been distracted by their relationship, but now that he wasn't around, and she was furious with him, it was easy to get lost in the world of logic and numbers. The fact that he had not reached out to her helped keep the idea of him away. It was Angie, one of the pool of assistants they shared, who let her know about the picture.

Camille was initially annoyed at the interruption, having immersed herself in the most recent coding issue wreaking havoc with their largest partner.

"Hey, Camille, you're friends with Jackson King, right? He's all over the internet!"

Camille squinted at the screen full of data. "Yes, Angie. He gets a lot of media attention."

"No, I mean, right now. Did you know about him and Kate Harlow?"

Camille's head snapped up. "What are you talking about?"

Angie pulled out her phone, scrolled for a few seconds, then pointed the screen at Camille.

There it was in full color. Jackson wrapped around a woman whose face was mostly buried in his neck. The remainder of her however, looked very much like Kate Harlow, award-winning actress and scandal queen. The headline read: *The mystery man behind Kate Harlow's messy divorce.*

Camille's mouth went so dry she could not speak. Angie backed out of her office stuttering about something Camille didn't try to understand.

Like the final puzzle piece, it all fit together. Her nagging fears, Jackson's silence, and of course, his father's prediction. Their relationship was a few weeks old and he was already unfaithful. It was humiliation on a globally public scale.

WHEN SHE WALKED into her apartment at the end of the day to find him sitting on her couch, Camille could not even scream. She had not anticipated seeing him for a very long time.

"Cam." He ran over to hug her, but she stepped out of his reach. "You're still mad at me."

"What are you doing here?"

"I just got back from LA, and I came straight here. I needed to see you. And tell you how sorry I am for what I said. I've been out of my mind. I feel like everything's in a big, twisted, jumbled mess. I can't make my way through it without you."

"Well, you're going to have to." Camille walked over to the coffee table and put her bags down.

"Why are you saying that? Because of my father?"

"I don't give a shit about your nonsense with your father. You two can go kill each other, for all I care. Manipulating me has been a pastime for both of you, and I'm done."

Jackson pulled the hair off his face, desperation darkening his expression. "Camille, I don't know where this is coming from. Please tell me what you mean."

"I mean he was right! Your father predicted your behavior to a T. I would never have expected that within minutes of saying goodbye to me, you'd be fucking around again. How long did it take Jackson? And you didn't even have the decency to stay behind closed doors. You had to get your face plastered all over the whole fucking internet!"

His fingers raked across the edge of his jaw, his eyes whipping from side to side. "I have no idea what you're talking about."

Sarcasm spilling from every word, she responded. "Really? Google yourself."

He pulled his phone out of his pocket. With a small number of clicks, swipes and taps, he appeared to discover some of the photos that Camille had seen earlier that day. "Holy shit. I had no idea…"

"Sucks getting caught, doesn't it?"

"Getting caught?" He walked over to stand directly in front of her. "What is it that you think I was doing?" There was not a touch of softness in his voice.

"It's pretty obvious, don't you think?"

"No, I don't. Why don't you tell me."

She wasn't going to back down, no matter how inscrutable he was being. "Well, clearly, you are fucking her."

"Clearly, huh? Okay. Let's say I'm fucking her." He bore down on her. "Why am I here? Why am I in your apartment right now, and not with her, fucking?"

Camille could not answer.

He bobbed his head. "So, it makes sense in your head that I

would profess my love to you, practically beg you to be with me, and then run off to screw some other woman?"

"Jackson, it looks-"

"I know what it looks like, Camille. You're just supposed to know better. I guess you and my father have more in common than I thought."

He was across the apartment and out the door before she could catch her breath.

CAMILLE HELD herself up by pushing down into the table behind her. She desperately wanted to sort the events of the past three days into right and wrong, but the tangle was unmanageable. In the *wrong* column was her accusation of his infidelity. He was right - she should have known better. That was not his style. There must have been another explanation. Also in the *wrong* column was what he said to her before he left for LA. Neither of them were in the clear.

Camille took her time to compose a message to him late that night.

Camille: I'd like to talk to you Jackson. Could you please meet me at Deluca's for lunch tomorrow?

Jackson: No.

Camille: Please.

Jackson: It will not serve us to be in an environment of forced civility. You know where I am and how to find me if you'd like to have a real conversation.

THE NEXT DAY she sat in her car, in front of his house, for twenty minutes, considering what she wanted out of this interaction with Jackson. Perhaps they were going to renegotiate their relationship, returning to their previous friendship. Perhaps this rift had shattered everything. This possibility created a ball of fire in her abdomen. Losing Jackson was not something she could survive. Especially after everything she'd already lost.

She entered the house using her key and called out to him. Jackson was nowhere to be found, and wasn't answering. She made her way from room to room until she heard clanging downstairs. *He must be in the gym.*

She saw him when she was halfway down the stairs, shirtless, hanging from the pull-up bar, earbuds in his ears, glistening with sweat. Every muscle of his back created a signature carving, like the finest sculpture. Camille knew that being just friends was never going to work. Not with the effect that a glimpse of his body had on hers.

He dropped down to the ground, bent over and picked up a bar loaded with weights. She made her way over to him and touched his back. He was in the middle of a lift, and nearly dropped the weights, startled by her appearance. He put the bar down and pulled out the earbuds.

"Cam. I didn't hear you. Sorry."

She bit her lower lip - hard - trying to stifle the tremor. "You're busy. I can come back later."

He clasped her wrist. "No! I'm glad you're here. Let me dry off and I'll meet you back upstairs. Pour yourself a glass of wine, if you like."

She glanced back at him, rubbing a towel over his face, as she ascended the stairs.

A glass of wine would do just fine.

He appeared in the kitchen as she was putting the cork back in the bottle. She had poured herself a very generous glass of the Italian red that was already open on his counter. He got a glass of water for himself.

"Should I jump in the shower?"

"No. I don't want to wait."

He nodded but didn't speak.

"I am incredibly uncomfortable right now, Jackson. I don't like this feeling. Not with you. Not ever."

"I understand. We're working with some intense material."

She gave him a look that she hoped communicated a lack of interest in him putting on his psychologist hat. "I'd like to speak with Jackson, my friend, and not Dr. King, please."

He took a big gulp of water. "Have I been demoted back to friend?"

"That's what we're here to talk about, isn't it?"

"I didn't know that was on the table, Camille."

A tired breath rushed from her body. She walked out of the kitchen and sat on the couch. "Tell me what happened in LA."

He joined her. "It's not something I should be talking about."

Her body stiffened. "Are you kidding me? How many millions of people saw those pictures, Jackson?!"

"She's a patient, Cam. I've been working with her and Jim on their reconciliation. I was at their house, and I think she was hugging me goodbye when those pictures were taken. I am absolutely not romantically involved with Kate Harlow. Or anybody else, for that matter." He looked up at her. "Except for you."

Camille pressed her lips together.

"Do you believe me, Cam?"

She took a sip of wine and a deep breath. "Yes, I do." It was a relief to say it.

He dropped his shoulders with a loud sigh. When he turned his head up to face her again, his expression was pained. "I've been thinking about what happened. Obsessively. I think we had parallel experiences."

"Please explain."

"Well, you know how you've had this idea of me as a

womanizer... you called me a man-whore once." Camille flinched with shame. "Then my father told you I would hurt you, that I wouldn't change my ways. So when you saw those pictures, the image was filtered through the idea of my being unfaithful and untrustworthy. I wanted you to trust what you knew about me, but maybe that was unfair. Maybe you could not have actually made a different assessment."

As usual, Jackson made perfect sense. "And your experience?"

"I had this idea that you and my father were colluding. You were having all these secret meetings that he was exaggerating and you were hiding. When you wouldn't let it go, I was just convinced he was in your ear. You had taken his side, and you would be rejecting me." He pulled at the whiskers on his chin. "Which you did."

"But I didn't."

"What you accused me of, Cam, was crushing."

"But you just explained how I didn't really have a choice. And please don't forget the numerous hateful things you said to me, Jack."

"You didn't deserve any of it. I admit that. The pain from my father just seeped out. You got hit by shrapnel."

"I don't believe that. I think that some of what you said to me, you believe to be true."

"You have to admit, Cam, you and my Dad have an unusually tight relationship. Everybody in the family knows that. Something about you is deeply... attractive... to him. I don't blame him, either. I feel the same way about you."

His exact words reverberated in her head. "Do you want me or pity me or something else?"

"Touche. Yes, that was unnecessarily mean. Point taken."

"I'm not trying to make a point, Jack. I'm trying to figure out what the hell happened. And what's going to happen."

"Are you here to dump me?"

"No."

He dropped his head into his hands with an audible sigh of relief. "Cam, I need you to believe that I would never, will never, betray you, physically or otherwise. Can you do that?"

So many disturbing images flashed in her head. So many possibilities. "I'll try my best."

"That's not very reassuring."

"It's the best I can do. For now."

His sadness nearly moved her to embrace him. But they still not had addressed the other major issue. "What are you going to do about your father? And no, I'm not colluding with him. I'm on your side. I always have been."

"We're going over there on Saturday."

"We?" No way was she going to be part of this.

"Yes, we. He specifically requested you be there. And I need you."

"I'm not going, Jackson. As you have been very open about, my presence is not helpful."

"Cam. Please. I'm asking you to come with me. Not because of him, but because it's going to be hell, and you're the only person in the world who can get me to screw my head back on when I've lost it. I realize what I'm asking you is the most self-ish, needy, inconsiderate thing I could ever do, and I'm asking anyway." He took her hands. "Please, Camille."

Her gaze moved from their hands, to his face, and back again. She did not consider herself a weak person, but saying no to a heartfelt request from Jackson was well out of her abilities.

CHAPTER 12

*J*ackson swerved around another car. Camille pressed her hand against the door, bracing her body. He was driving too aggressively, but she didn't dare admonish him. The tension in his body filled the air around him with electricity. She was scared, but his fear felt even bigger. The enmity between father and son was not news to Camille. She just had no idea how they were going to solve a lifetime's worth of issues in one afternoon. And how the hell she was going to survive the certain warfare.

They pulled into the driveway, but neither made a move to exit the car. Jackson turned to Camille, and took her face in his hands. "Cam, please listen to me. No matter what happens here tonight, no matter what is said, you need to keep one thing in mind. You are the love of my life. I am so grateful for you it makes me tongue-tied. I don't want anything that is said here today to be translated in your mind into anything other than those ideas. Do you understand?"

She stared into his unblinking gaze, his thumbs stroking her cheeks. This was one of the strangest requests she had ever received, one which made a cascade of chills run up and down her spine. "Yes, I understand."

Elena King greeted them at the door with hugs that lingered too long. She looked like she had been crying.

"I'm so glad you're here, Jackson. This situation has been the most terrible thing that has ever happened to this family."

Camille's very unkind thought was: Lucky them.

Elena squeezed Camille's shoulders. "Camille, my darling. I can't thank you enough for coming. I know this must be hard. Dealing with someone else's family drama."

"It's okay, Mrs. King. I'm happy to be here for Jackson."

Jonathan was filling two tumblers with Scotch when they walked into the living room. He greeted them with a simple nod, then handed one of the glasses to his son.

"No thank you, Dad. I'm driving."

Before Jonathan could put the glass down, Camille offered her hand. "I'll take it, thank you."

His eyebrows vaulted upward. "Excellent."

"Can I get you two anything to eat?" Elena offered.

Both she and Jackson shook their heads. Food was the last thing on their minds. Elena went into the kitchen anyway, disregarding their answer.

NEITHER MAN WAS one for small talk, so when Elena returned from the kitchen with a tray of cheese and crackers, Jonathan spoke. "Shall we begin?"

"Of course."

"First, I want to apologize for my misstep with Camille. It was inappropriate for me to go to her privately about you. I just thought we had a relationship-"

"Stop right there. You don't have the right to intrude in my private affairs. Even if you think you two have a *relationship*." Jackson's face twisted into a snarl on the last word.

"Affairs is the right word." The presumptuous King glare took over Jonathan's face.

"Why don't you just come out and say what you want to

COLLECTING SECRETS | 133

say, Dad? Let's not waste any more time." Jackson was sitting so far forward in his seat, Camille feared he might fall over.

"By the time I was your age, I was married with four children, had a good job, a stable life. I wasn't running around like a teenager begging for attention. My priorities were my family."

"You know what you didn't have, Dad? A PhD, two New York Times bestsellers, and an invitation into the homes of celebrities and world leaders."

"That's the problem, Jackson. You've amassed several formidable accomplishments, but they're all tainted by a complete lack of decorum."

Camille was relieved when Jackson laughed at this comment. Better than screaming, perhaps.

"Lack of decorum, you say? Hmmmm…"

"Yes. You are a grown man, but you run around like a twenty-year-old playboy who is not serious about his life. You act like you have no responsibilities, and bear no consequence for the damage you cause."

"Meaning what?" Jackson's composure was outmatched only by the steel in his voice.

"It was a matter of days between the time you stood here, at *my* dinner table, and announced your relationship with Camille and your appearance in a highly unflattering way with some famous actress."

Camille saw Jackson shudder and then recover.

"That's between Camille and me, don't you think? How is it any of your business?"

"Because someone has to look out for her. The stature of her family, and the exemplary life she has built, does not need to be diminished by your carelessness."

Elena reached out and took Camille's hand, but neither shifted their focus from the two men battling it out in front of them.

"Since when are you her guardian? The protector of her

family name? You realize you're not actually her father, right? She is not your daughter!"

The elder pointed directly at his son. "She could have been! She could easily have been the daughter we lost!"

Elena stood up so quickly, she forgot Camille's hand was still in hers, and she yanked them both up. "Jonathan!" The beautiful, consistently composed woman had turned a frightening shade of red and was panting.

It was impossible for Camille to process.

Jonathan immediately dropped his battle stance. "Darling... I'm so sorry... I did not mean to..."

"How could you, Jonathan?" Elena sat down, and again brought Camille, who had no idea what was going on, with her.

Thankfully, Jackson spoke. "Can somebody please tell me what the hell is going on?"

Neither parent broke the silence, until Elena began to cry. Her husband put his hands on her shoulders, and addressed the others. "That was out of line. I shouldn't have said that. I apologize."

"Dad, what did you mean? What are you talking about?"

Elena looked up at her husband with a combination of pain and anger. "You've done it now Jonathan. Now you get to explain yourself."

Jonathan cleared his throat. "Before you were born, Jackson, we had another child. A daughter. She was born too early and only lived three days."

Both Jackson's and Camille's mouths dropped open.

"I had made a promise to your mother that we would never speak of it, and I have just broken her confidence. I feel deeply sorry." He wiped the tears from his wife's face. "Will you ever forgive me?"

Camille had never heard his voice so filled with softness.

"Wait a minute." All attention moved to Jackson. "Mom, I can see that this is extremely painful for you. But it's also important that we discuss this. Secrets like this create toxicity in relationships that can destroy families."

Camille winced, knowing how much everyone hated when Dr. King, world famous psychologist, entered the room.

"Her name was Violet." Somehow that statement, from Elena King, cleared the room of any previous tension. "Losing her was the single most painful thing I have ever gone through. I almost didn't make it." She looked up at her husband. "We almost didn't make it."

"Tell me what you mean."

Camille was stunned that everyone was going along with Jackson's line of questions. She wondered if he had hypnotized them.

"I was still grieving when I got pregnant with you and I went crazy after you were born. I couldn't stand the idea of anything happening to you, so you became my whole life. I neglected myself, I neglected your father, I barely functioned." She turned to address her son, directly. "I don't know about all this psychology stuff, Jackson. But I think your father never forgave you for that."

Camille saw a tightening around Jackson's jaw. Jonathan dropped onto the arm of the couch next to his wife. "Elena…"

"I think it's true, Jonathan. You were angry with me for abandoning you. And maybe you were right. But I wasn't in my right mind. All I could think about was keeping our baby safe."

The truth presented itself like an unfolding flower. It all began to make sense to Camille - Jackson's unusual closeness to his mother, the enmity with his father, Jonathan's interest in her…

"Camille…"

She jumped at the sound of her name from Elena's lips. "Yes, Mrs. King."

"It has been an absolute delight having you as part of our family. I can't tell you how much we have appreciated your presence. And how much we love you. But I think that when you came into our lives, Jonathan saw you as Violet. I know that you are exactly the daughter he thought he would have. I'm sorry if it felt overbearing or uncomfortable. He wasn't trying to hurt you."

Camille shook her head briskly. "No, Mrs. King, it hasn't been any of those things. I love you too. Being part of your family has been a wonderful experience. I'm sure I will never be able to thank you enough for everything you've done for me."

"It was nothing, Camille. We did nothing. I wish I could have done more."

"What would you have done, Dad?"

Camille could not tell what sentiment guided that question, whether it was interest or blame.

"Jackson, I don't think you understand the enormity of the tragedy this young lady faced. Most people don't recover from things like that. Your mother and I barely did. But she showed us all what dignity and grace and courage look like."

"Don't you think I understand that? Camille has been the most important person in my adult life."

"I don't think you do, son. You treat her like she's a regular person. She's not. She's an extraordinary person. She deserves more respect, more thoughtfulness, more care and consideration. She is not one of your one-night-stand bikini models."

It was surreal, being discussed as if she was not there, and Camille felt herself pull away.

"Don't you think I know that?! This is the woman I want to spend the rest of my life with. There is nothing I wouldn't do for her."

Camille snapped out of her daze. "Gentlemen-"

The elder cut her off. "Jackson, you have lived a blessed life. You have never known real tragedy."

"I haven't known tragedy? Aren't we forgetting something, Dad?"

"A mistake devoid of consequence is not a tragedy. And this is not the time or place to bring up... the past."

Camille wracked her mind to make sense of Jonathan's comment. What was he talking about?

He paused, bringing his index finger to rest below his lower lip, the King family pose for deep thinking, and then continued. "There are events that forever alter your view of the world. I know what it's like to lose a child. And I know what it's like to almost lose the woman I love. I just don't think you would survive it if you continued on this course and Camille was forced to leave you."

The two men locked eyes as if they had only just seen each other for the first time. Jackson worked his jaw while he considered his next words.

"You're right, Dad. I can't imagine a life without Camille in it. And you're also right that my life has been magical, for the most part. With a couple of significant exceptions. You have provided for all of us very well. But you just didn't give a shit. At least not about me."

"Jackson!" His mother had shifted from sadness to shock.

His father, however, had no reaction at all. "I'm sorry you feel that way, Jackson. It's not true that I didn't care. It might have been true that I cared too much."

"Dad, I know that I didn't follow the path you wanted me to. And the life I lead is a bit too flashy for your tastes. But you have to admit that I have done fairly well. And you have never, not even once, indicated that you were proud of me. Or that you respect, from one man to another, what I have accomplished. Would that have been so hard?" The tiniest sliver of vulnerability created a crack in Jackson's voice.

Camille wanted to wrap her arms around this man, who had always been a pillar of strength for her, and had been carrying this level of hurt and rejection. Instead she gripped his hand, praying he could feel how much she loved him.

"I don't have an adequate answer for you, son. Perhaps your mother is right, and I was still holding on to what happened at the beginning of your life. I'm not certain. But I do know that I have never been more proud of anyone than I have been of you. When I push, it's because I see how much further you can go, how greatly your accomplishments will dwarf mine. You are my beloved son. I would never want you to experience the losses that I have."

Camille stroked the back of Jackson's neck which released tension beneath her touch. She had no idea how emotional this was going to be. She had anticipated yelling and screaming from these powerhouses, but this heartfelt conversation was shattering her.

Jackson stood up and everyone froze. "This has been helpful. Thank you. We're going to go now."

"Jackson," his mother implored, "don't go just yet. Why don't you two stay the night? You're coming back here tomorrow for Sunday dinner anyway, right?"

"Thanks, Mom, but we're going to go. I have a lot to think about."

Jonathan walked over to his son. "I'm sorry, Jackson. I made some important mistakes." He clasped his son tightly.

When the men separated, Jackson remained steely. "We all have, Dad."

THEY HARDLY SPOKE during the drive home, except to decide at whose house they would spend the night. Camille knew that Jackson needed time to digest what had just happened, and let him sit on the couch uninterrupted while she sorted out the plans for dinner.

He patted the space next to him. "Come sit with me, Cam."

"Of course, honey."

She kissed him, not knowing how else to shift the sadness in his eyes.

"Thanks for being there with me today. I'm sorry for how much we entangled you in our mess. No one should ever have to go through that."

"I'm glad I could be there for you. And I was the only one who got out of there unscathed. You all were insanely kind to me."

"I meant everything I said, Cam. I hope you know that."

I want to spend the rest of my life with her. Camille could not forget those words if she wanted to. Which she didn't. "I do."

She ran her thumb across the crease on his forehead. "What can I do for you? Would you like to talk about what happened? Would you like to do something to take your mind off it?" She didn't necessarily mean it enticingly, but perhaps it wasn't a bad idea.

"Actually, there is something I'd like to discuss."

She waited for him to continue.

"One of the points my father made hit home. I think I have been a bit too casual about us. I take it for granted that you will always be here, with me. I assume my certainty and commitment should necessarily translate to your certainty and commitment. But that doesn't respect and honor you. I don't want you to ever question that you are a priority for me."

Camille had no idea where this was going, which left her feeling unsettled instead of clear. "Thanks for saying that. I know you're here for me."

"I don't want to be apart from you. I want you to move in here, with me."

Her heart skipped a beat. Before she could respond, he continued.

"I've just been looking at this place, and although I think it's big enough, I'm not sure it's laid out well for you to have spaces you consider your own. We could remodel. I've been thinking about updating the kitchen anyway, and the guest suite. I think you could do it, and have it exactly how you want."

For the first time that day, Jackson looked hopeful. Happy even. But this was not comforting to Camille. "Jackson, I would love to talk to you about this, but I'm not sure now is the time, especially considering what's going on with your family. Maybe we should focus on what's happening now."

"Cam, there's nothing more important than our future. There's nothing I can do about what's happened with my father. But I heard him clearly about taking our relationship seriously. And I want to do that. I want to talk about the next step for us."

Camille steadied herself. "I want to make sure you're not bypassing, Jackson. We're in the middle of something huge for your family. Is it really the time to plan remodeling your house and my moving in?"

"Yes. It is."

She nodded slowly, knowing she had limited ability to change his train of thought. "Okay, then."

"Good. So what do you think?"

"In theory, I would be happy to move in. There are a bunch of logistics to sort out, including my apartment, and our financial arrangement."

"I think it would probably be a good idea to keep your place, so we could stay there during construction. Then, we could sublet, or let it go, whatever you feel comfortable with. I don't know what you mean by financial arrangement."

"Well, how would you like me to participate in paying for the house, or the construction, or bills?"

His eyes narrowed. "I am not asking you for anything, financially. I'm fully able to take care of both of us."

"I know you're able to, but it doesn't mean you should. We've never spoken about this, but maybe we need to. We're not in your parents' era anymore. I don't expect you to support me."

"I'm not trying to revive some antiquated fifties concept of partnership, but I don't see any reason for you to pay for anything. Which is not a commentary on your ability to fully support yourself, which I know you can."

The doorbell was a welcome break of the tension.

Jackson stood up. "Dinner's here. Let's eat and we can talk about this later."

THEY SAT AT THE TABLE, plates half full with the dinner that neither felt like eating.

Jackson moved a broccoli floret across his plate. "So, when would you like to move? I can get the movers there as soon as you like."

Tightness gripped her abdomen. "Jackson, I can't do this. I can't make these plans with everything else so unsettled. It's not working for me."

He tapped his fork on the side of the plate. "Okay, Cam. What would you like to talk about?"

"How do you feel about what happened with your family today?"

He exhaled. "I feel upset and confused. I feel compassion for what my parents went through, and have a better understanding of what created their beliefs and behaviors, but I don't know what to do with my father. I don't know how to make our relationship going forward better than our relationship in the past. I don't know if that's even a possibility."

"Is there anything that would make you feel better?"

"Talking about something else. Like you moving in."

"You're relentless, Jackson King." The tiniest smile made its way into her expression.

"No argument there. But you know me, Cam. I'm as good about all of this as can be expected. Don't you agree?"

Camille took a moment to look at him. He was right. His behavior seemed integrated and solid. "Alright. I'll let it go for now. We can talk about whatever you want."

"Let's talk about money. We never really have, and maybe it needs to be explicit now. I know you are quite capable of supporting yourself. You don't need me. But my taking on the financial responsibility for our shared household is a hard line for me. I wouldn't be honest if I told you this was negotiable. It's not. Can you be okay with that?"

Camille knew that Jackson had very few hard lines. She would honor this one, even if she kept in the back of her mind that she might have more negotiating power later in their relationship. This wasn't the end of their discussions about money. "Yes, I can. And I want you to know that I appreciate your generosity. I understand the intent behind it."

"Good. And it's my pleasure, love. There isn't anything I wouldn't do for you."

She couldn't quite get her face to smile the way she wanted it to, tightness pulling along her jawline. She tried to relax, unsure why she was still feeling so unsettled.

Another disturbing thought entered her mind. "Have you thought about if we're going to Sunday dinner?"

"I'm back and forth on it. What do you think?"

"This has to be your decision, Jack. Your stakes are higher than mine."

"I feel like we should go."

"I'm glad to hear you say that. I'm here for you."

"I know, love."

It could have almost been mistaken for any of the Sunday dinners they'd had for years. Justin was bored, Julian was awkward, Jenna was frustrated with the rowdy class of seventh graders she'd been assigned. But Camille noticed all the undercurrents: Mrs. King's over exuberance and exaggerated cheerfulness, Mr. King's solemn expressions, and Jackson's unyielding grip on her hand.

She couldn't wait to get back home. The tension, subtle as it was, had created soreness around her shoulders. They were nearly out the door when Mr. King asked them to join him in his office.

He stepped behind his over-sized desk but didn't sit down.

"I am very happy you came to dinner today. It would not have been the same without you."

Camille looked up at Jackson with a silent urge to say something nice.

"Thanks, Dad. I'm glad we came as well."

"I'm sure you know that I am happy you have made a commitment to building a home together. You young people seem to think marriage is outdated, but I realize this is your version of it. I'd like to help the two of you, even though you haven't asked for it."

"I don't know what you mean, Dad."

Mr. King proceeded to open a large, leather portfolio, and write something. When he tore out a section of paper, Camille realized he had just written a check. Jackson's body stiffened.

"I don't know exactly what the remodel will cost, but here's something to start. This is for the both of you."

Camille swallowed, afraid that their fighting would begin again.

"Dad, I don't need -"

Camille squeezed his forearm, stopping the rejection she knew was coming. She spoke so softly he had to lean in to hear her. "Jackson, you said you would do anything for me. I need you to accept that check from your father. Please."

His eyes darted from side to side as he considered his options and processed her request.

When Jackson stepped across the room to take the check from his father's outstretched hand, Camille let herself take a deep exhale.

They were nearly home when the right words formed. "Jackson, I have never felt prouder of you than I do right now. Thank you for doing this."

He didn't turn away from the windshield. "I promised you anything, Cam. I meant it."

"I love you, Jackson. You are my hero."

• • •

IT WASN'T until they were getting ready for bed, and Jackson emptied his pockets, including the check he had folded and put away without looking at, that the day's events became clear. The look on Jackson's face brought Camille to his side, concerned. He handed her the check.

"Holy shit!" Camille's hand began to shake. "Your father gave us a check for a hundred thousand dollars. Made out to both of us." She thought maybe saying it aloud would reveal that she had misread the check.

"We can't accept this, Cam."

"I…" She really didn't know what to say.

"I'm not going to cash this check."

"Wait a minute, Jack. Let's not make a decision right now. We'll be able to think more clearly in a few days." She put the check down on the table as if it were covered in poison.

CHAPTER 13

*C*amille sat on the floor in the overcrowded living room. It had been nearly six weeks of living with Jackson, and all their stuff, in her tiny house. Sitting on the couch provided too much perspective into the chaos of boxes and belongings, so she'd taken to bringing herself down, below the disaster. Perhaps she'd been wrong to refuse Jackson's multiple offers to rent a hotel suite while his house - their house - was being renovated. It just seemed so frivolous. Especially considering she had a perfectly fine living space.

The memory of the day, so many years ago, when she moved out of the first house they all shared, had gone hazy. It had been one of the most painful days of her life, one of the few in which she honestly considered that Jackson King might not be a part of her future, even as a friend. His habits had made it too difficult to share space. But now they'd spent weeks on top of each other, in every possible way, and she only loved him more.

The disorganization and mess were an entirely different matter. They had weeks, maybe months, before they could move and she wasn't sure she could take it. She just didn't function well in chaos.

An unrecognized number appeared on her phone. "Hello. This is Camille."

SHE SAT FROZEN, hunched over her phone, mouth open, well after the end of the call.

"Cam, what's wrong?"

Jackson had just entered the house. She couldn't look up or away from her phone screen despite the fact that it held no information other than the smiling face of the man who was standing above her.

"I just got the strangest phone call, Jack. I have to go down to the police station. Something's going on about my parents."

He dropped down to his knees. "Your parents? Who died thirteen years ago? What is this about?"

"I don't know. But I need to go find out."

"Now?"

"Yes. Now."

He helped her up and led her to the door. "I'm coming with you."

They were greeted by two burly officers at the station and led to a conference room that looked more like a large jail cell than a place for conversation. Camille distracted herself by examining the cracked walls, peeling paint, and trying to ignore the industrial smell. She expected to find the large two-way mirror she always saw in police shows, but there wasn't one. The introductions began with the handful of men in suits - FBI, apparently - and continued with the men in police uniforms. There were five of them, total.

Jackson spoke first. "Can someone please tell us what's going on here? This is obviously very upsetting for my girlfriend."

Camille looked over at him. God, she loved how strong he was.

The one who introduced himself as Agent Sawyer answered. "Yes. We appreciate you coming down here. The Bureau is working on a joint case with the SFPD and we think you may be able to help."

"You said on the phone this has something to do with my parents. That was so long ago. I don't understand."

Sergeant Williams spoke next. "Ms. Moreau... we're going to start at the beginning."

Camille braced herself.

"We recently came upon some information that sheds a new light on your parents' death."

Ice filled the center of her chest. "How could that be? They had an accident? What other information could there be?"

"Ms. Moreau-"

"Please call me Camille."

"Fine. Camille. We believe your parents were murdered."

She jerked back, hitting the chair so hard it screeched across the concrete floor.

Jackson sprung up and placed his hands on her shoulders. "You better have a damn good reason for saying something like that."

"Mr. King-"

"It's *Doctor* King."

"Yes, well, Dr. King. We have evidence." The sergeant looked over at Camille, quickly wiped the concerned look from his face, and cleared his throat. "Approximately eighteen months ago, a man currently in custody made allegations about a crime scheme that permeated the highest levels of city governance. We've been investigating his claims, most of which have been substantiated."

Williams paused again and pressed his lips tightly together. His eyes shifted from one of his colleagues to another. "We were informed about an organized crime ring and their attempts to subvert the judicial system. Records reveal hundreds of payments made to some of the city's top officials. Politicians, administrators, judges."

Camille flinched at the last word, not wanting to hear what she already knew was coming next.

"Your father's name was on that list."

Her gasp was partially stifled by her own hands flying up to her mouth.

"Allegedly, several judges took significant amounts of money for throwing trials. Your father's name appeared on the ledgers for many years. And then something happened."

Camille swallowed against the violent urge to throw up.

"What happened?" Jackson never let up his grip on Camille, while projecting his voice to fill the large room.

"He tried to stop. We found communications that indicated he wanted out. He was in the middle of a high profile case and refused to deliver a false verdict. We believe he was killed to remove him from presiding over the case."

"No!" Camille's body shot up, almost knocking Jackson over. "They died in an accident. He was flying the plane that they crashed in. It was an accident. And none of that stuff you said about him is true. It's not true!!"

Another officer spoke. "Ms. Moreau, we understand this might be upsetting-"

"Are you kidding me? It's not upsetting, because none of it is true." The hysteria in her voice stood in stark contrast to her false words.

They all nodded at her. Sergeant Williams continued. "Unfortunately, we strongly believe it is all true."

Jackson gently led Camille back to her seat. "What do you want from us? Why are we here? Clearly my girlfriend knows nothing about this."

Agent Sawyer raised his hand to stop the officers from speaking. "We need your help."

"How can I possibly help with something I know nothing

about?" If not for Jackson's steady hands, the tremor through her body might have vaulted her off the cold, metal chair.

"The evidence is significant. Enough to put many people behind bars. But there's more. And we believe you have it."

"I don't have anything. What are you talking about?"

"That letter from your father also indicated that he held on to the most damning evidence, as leverage. We believe he could lead us to the people at the top of this scheme. The ones we haven't yet been able to name."

Jackson aimed all of his attention toward Sawyer. "How could she possibly have this evidence? She has nothing to do with any of this."

"It's with his things." She spoke with a breathy monotone. "It's with their things, isn't it?"

A different, deeper voice, responded. "We believe so, Camille."

"I can tell you where those things are." The storage locker whose bills she paid, but that she had never entered or examined. She stood up. "Can I leave now? Are we done?"

Agent Sawyer's stoic expression flashed to the quickest smile she had ever seen. "We appreciate your cooperation. This is incredibly helpful. There's something else, however."

Camille swayed, catching herself with a hand on the back of the chair.

"You might want to sit down, ma'am."

Camille glanced at Jackson, who bowed his head toward the seat. He remained standing behind her.

"The people behind this… they're very dangerous. They have a lot to lose by us finding this information. They might retaliate."

Jackson slapped his palms onto the table. "Are you telling me that we are in danger? That Camille is in danger?"

Camille blinked the thoughts away.

"It is a possibility, Dr. King. We are willing to provide you with full protective detail if needed."

Camille shook her head. "This is not happening."

Williams leaned in toward her. She could almost see compassion in his eyes. "Ms. Moreau, the threat of danger is low. But we want to make sure you're safe. We believe this case extends far and deep into the local judicial and governing bodies. It's hard to know who to trust. It's best to be completely safe."

"Holy shit." All the breath left her body.

Jackson ran his hand down the back of her hair. "How long do you think this is going to last?"

"It's hard to say, Dr. King. It depends how quickly we can find what we're looking for."

Jackson walked around to the stack of papers on the metal desk. "I hope you realize how much you're asking. We have a good life. A beautiful life. It's bad enough that Camille had to go through this horrible tragedy. Now you're taking her through hell again."

Camille reached out for his hand. "It's okay, Jackson. I can handle it."

"You shouldn't have to." His voice cracked

Both Sawyer and Williams put out their hands. "We appreciate your cooperation."

CAMILLE MADE it all the way through the station, the drive home and into bed before allowing the rush of fear, grief, and rage to overcome her. Jackson held her through the night as she sobbed. By the time light filled the room, the tears had dried and an idea solidified itself in her mind.

She waited until Jackson began to stir. She was glad he had slept, even though she had not. "I have to get rid of the money."

"Cam, what are you saying?"

"That money my parents left me. It's from my father's crimes. I don't want it."

He rubbed the sleep from his eyes. "What do you want to do?"

"I'm not sure. I don't care. Burn it all, maybe."

"Cam, it's impractical to burn millions of dollars. And wasteful. It could be put to great use in this world."

"But it's dirty, Jack. Tainted." The tears began again. The father she thought she knew had been replaced by a despicable criminal.

"I understand, love. I think we have some urgent things to decide. What to do with the money is perhaps secondary." He waited for a sign she had heard him. "We have to keep you safe."

She burrowed more deeply into his side. She couldn't imagine not being safe in his arms. "I'm not afraid, Jack."

"I know, love. But I'm not taking any chances." He tilted her chin upwards to look at him. "Let's go away. Anywhere you want - Italy, Thailand, Brazil. Anything."

"I don't want to run away from this. I don't want this ridiculous threat to turn my life upside down."

"Let's not think about it that way. Let's think about it like a well-deserved vacation. You've been working so hard and I've been wrapped up with the new book. We're managing a home remodel. We haven't had a minute. We've earned this."

"I'll think about it. If you promise to not dismiss my ideas about getting rid of the money."

"You have a deal, Cam. And I'll even take it further. I have a friend who consults with big companies about charitable giving. I'll get in touch with her and get some information on how we can distribute this money. How does that sound?"

Camille bit the side of her lip. "Are you upset, Jack? It might be selfish of me to not want to keep it… for us."

"That was only ever your money, Cam. I support whatever you want to do with it. Our future never involved any of it."

She made herself relax. "Thank you. I'll think about where I'd like to go."

"Great." His body softly molded itself around her.

"And I never, ever want to go back to that station again. Ever."

"I will do everything I can to make sure you never have to."

Her eyes closed heavily. Relief brought fatigue, but her body had a different plan. Her hand slid around to cup his bottom and press him into her. "There's something else I think might help."

"Yes, please."

"WHO WOULD you like to help, Camille? What would you like your money to do?"

Ramona had a nice face. Camille knew she would be beautiful. She had dated Jackson, of course. But she was much kinder, and much less arrogant than the women Camille had gotten used to seeing around him.

They had decided to sit outside at a cafe, taking advantage of an unexpectedly warm day. It felt good to get out of the house.

"I'm not sure, Ramona. I was hoping you could help."

"Absolutely. Glad to help." Ramona squeezed her hand. "First thing to sort out are the categories of charities you're interested in. There are many to choose from - hunger, clean water, medical research, human trafficking…"

Camille couldn't hold back a grimace.

"Don't worry. There are also hundreds of organizations that support the arts, music, dance, education."

Camille relaxed. "First thing that comes to mind is something with kids. I know there are organizations that teach girls to code. I'd love to support that. And women's shelters. And maybe homelessness."

"That's a great start. Why don't you send me your thoughts, and I'll compile a list of possibilities. With the amount of money you're ready to donate, you're going to do a great deal of good."

"I hope so. That's the whole point of this." Camille pushed down the encroaching sadness.

"Listen, I don't want to overstep, but Jackson told me a bit about your... situation."

Embarrassment flushed her cheeks. Her father being a criminal wasn't something she wanted anyone to know.

Ramona smiled so sweetly, it was impossible for Camille to assume judgment on her part. "There might be another way to approach this."

"Okay..."

"Have you thought about restitution? About helping out the individuals, or organizations that support those individuals, directly? In cases like this, when the money has deep significance, it can help to know that you've provided a matching counter to whatever harmful act occurred. It can still be anonymous, which I would recommend, but you would know. And it might help you heal."

Camille could've fallen in love with the woman sitting across from her. That was a brilliant idea. Exactly what she was looking for. But...

She tilted her head. "How would that work? I mean, I don't know who was harmed."

"I would assume that most of the cases are now public record. It would take some work, but you could find them."

Understanding the possibilities, Camille's eyes opened wide. "Yes. You're right!"

"It's not strictly my area, but I've got lots of connections who can assist you. I'd love to help make this happen."

"Wow."

"I'm going to be away for the next week or so. Heading to the east coast for some family stuff. I might not be as accessible as usual, but I can take care of anything you need when I get back."

Camille wanted to spring up and give this woman a big hug. She kept herself in her seat. "My gosh, Ramona, I can't thank you enough. You've already been so helpful. And kind. I've known most of Jackson's exes, and I can't think of a single one who would be this great."

"Well, you've got to stop thinking about me as Jackson's ex. We hardly dated. And that was back in college, a million years ago. I've been hearing about you for so long. I'm glad we finally had a chance to meet."

This time, Camille followed her instinct and walked to the other side of the table and gave her new friend a deep hug.

Camille opened the door at home to a view that made everything better. Jackson, wearing his Kiss the Chef apron, creating wonderful sights and smells in the kitchen.

He greeted her with a soft smile. "Hello, love."

She gave him a kiss that raised the temperature in the already steamy kitchen by a few degrees.

"Mmmmm. That was nice. How was your meeting with Ramona?"

"Good. I love her. She was so nice. And helpful."

"You sound surprised. Expecting something else?"

"You forget that I've met all your ex-girlfriends, darling." She winked at him.

"Touché. So, what did you two decide?"

"She had the best idea. I think I want to help some of the victims of my father's schemes. Lots of people got screwed. Maybe I can make some of it right again. She called it restitution."

Jackson's eyes doubled in size. "Cam, that sounds... ambitious."

"I know. But I have some ideas and Ramona's going to help.

How hard could it be finding out who was involved in his cases?"

Jackson shook his head. "Cam, you know I'm behind you for any and all of this. But this idea sounds too dangerous. Don't forget that each of these cases was a crime being covered up. Digging around might piss off the wrong people."

"I told you, Jack. I won't let myself be frightened by this."

CHAPTER 14

TWELVE YEARS EARLIER

"*A*re you still celebrating?" Jonathan King's tone, thick with judgment, translated across the phone line.

"Yes, Dad. Twenty-one is a big deal. It only happens once."

"You need to act responsibly, Jackson. You're an adult now. It's time to leave your teenage antics behind."

"Yes, sir." There was little attempt to hide his sarcasm.

"I'll expect you on time for Sunday dinner tomorrow."

"As usual, Dad. Good night." Jackson happily accepted the tequila shot handed to him by his buddy and threw it back. He was glad he'd sprung for the good stuff.

It had been a week full of parties to celebrate his twenty-first birthday, which had culminated in his friends taking over their favorite bar. He had always been able to handle his liquor. So well, in fact, that at the end of the long night, Jackson was the least drunk of all of his friends, and volunteered to drive a few of them home.

After dropping off the last of his passengers, Jackson congratulated himself on a job well done. His father's reproachful voice brought a sneer to his face. That man didn't know anything. Jackson could party with the best of them and still get everyone home safely. He looked down to turn up the radio. His favorite song was playing.

When Jackson woke up in the hospital, he had lost five hours of his memory. The person he hit as he had drifted into oncoming traffic had nearly lost her life.

The next six months of his life, as he prepared to finish college and begin a prestigious fellowship across the country, were spent navigating the judicial system. There had been civil and criminal charges. Thankfully, the driver of the other car had a successful recovery. And then, one day, the whole thing went away. His father, who had been managing the situation from the beginning, ordered him to never speak of the accident again. Jackson was too afraid not to obey.

Now

Any time Camille could sneak out of work, she headed down to the state and county offices, trying to find records of all her father's court cases. A lawyer friend of Jackson's helped with the especially difficult ones, as did Ramona's contacts at the county clerk. After ten days she'd assembled hundreds of pages of copies which covered her entire dining table. Then began the work of figuring out if anything had criminal elements.

Camille realized, while looking over the huge pile of legal documents, that she didn't actually have a plan. There was no way of knowing, without reading through all the court proceedings, which way the verdict had been swayed. She had thought that just finding all the cases ending with a not guilty verdict would point to wronged plaintiffs. Skimming the briefs revealed that that was clearly incorrect. And many of the cases didn't have individual plaintiffs. They originated from the city or state. The idea of restitution began to feel more and more like folly.

She dropped her head onto the table, the probability of defeat lodging itself firmly into her awareness.

No.

She would not be thwarted this easily. She lifted her head, picked up the next folder in the pile and flipped it open. She'd gotten used to the strange format of these documents and her eyes went straight to the section naming the plaintiff and defendant.

County of Santa Clara vs. King, Jackson.

She stared at those seven words until the burning of her eyes forced her to blink. She lifted the dozen or so pages from the others, slid over to her right, where there was an open spot on the table, and began to read. Every single word.

She'd only just finished when Jackson came breezing into the house all smiles and excitement.

"Hey Cam, did you see the interview?"

She'd completely forgotten that he was being interviewed by the local news station. "No."

He stopped walking toward her, his smile flattening into worry. "What's wrong, baby? Is all that legal stuff too hard to deal with?"

"No. I mean yes. I mean..." She looked him squarely in the face, trying to orient what she'd just read with the man standing in front of her. She stretched out her arm, clutching the documents, toward him. "I need you to explain this."

He took the pile and read. Confusion quickly turned to recognition, then something that, on another face, might have been called shame. But Jackson King didn't feel shame. At least not in the decade she'd known him.

He dropped the papers on the table, walked into the kitchen, opened a bottle of wine, and returned with the bottle and two glasses. He filled them both before speaking.

"I turned twenty-one in the middle of senior year. I had

already gotten into the program at Columbia. Life was really great." He took three gulps of wine, then refilled his glass.

"My buddies took me out to celebrate. I was the most sober and I drove everyone home. Safely. But right before I got home, I drifted into the center of the highway and hit another car." He looked directly at her. "Actually, that part I don't remember, but that's what they told me happened."

Camille counted her breaths while waiting for him to continue.

"I hit a woman, coming home from work. A waitress, if I remember. Both cars were totaled but our injuries weren't too bad. I had a concussion and fractured my collarbone. She broke a few bones. We were lucky."

Camille pulled the stack of papers toward her and stared down at them, desperately hoping that something reasonable would emerge. "Why did it go to court?"

"They did a breathalyzer on me at the hospital, and it showed I was over the limit. Because of the severity of the accident, the county had to press charges." It was only at that point that shock entered his expression.

"Holy shit, Cam. Your father was the judge?"

She nodded. He swallowed.

"What happened to the case?"

"My father took charge of everything. He told me he convinced the woman to drop the civil suit, hired me the best attorneys and got the criminal case closed. He kept me out of it, so that I could focus on school. Then, I don't know, it all just disappeared. As if it had never happened."

It was her turn to wipe out her glass of wine.

Fear blazed in his eyes. "You don't think…"

"I think there's only one person who would know that answer."

He pulled his phone from his jacket pocket and began vigorously typing and swiping.

This was so confusing. "What are you doing?"

"I'm booking a ride to my parent's house. Not going to drive after that glass of wine. Especially not after…"

She touched his arm with her fingertips, which caused him to whip his head up.

"Things are already pretty tense with your Dad. Maybe you should give it a minute before storming down there."

His head bobbed up and down. "I understand why you'd say that. But I'm not going to wait."

"This isn't news, Jackson. This was twelve years ago. Another day or two isn't going to change what happened."

As if it were possible, the line of his jaw sharpened. "There's no reason to wait, Cam."

He stood up and walked toward the bathroom. "The car will be here in ten minutes."

THEY SAT in the backseat of the SUV, both staring straight ahead. This entanglement between the most important men in her life was not settling into a coherent story. Could it really be possible that her father, the man who'd become like a father to her, and the man she loved, all conspired in covering up a crime? Devastation molded itself into an expression of horror.

Jackson turned to her as they passed the first gate of his parent's property.

"Thanks for coming."

"Of cou-"

He touched her cheek. "And I have to say that the way you looked at me today is something I never, ever, want to experience in my life again. You have every right to be horrified. But I promise you, whatever happened here, I will make it right."

JACKSON strode directly into the sitting room, where he knew his father would be spending the evening. "What did you do, Dad? With my DUI case?"

The elder King stared at his son, then pulled at the lapels of his jacket. "I made it go away. I saved your future."

The two men stood, immobile and unspeaking, until Camille couldn't stand the silence one more second. "How did you make it go away, Mr. King? How did this involve my father?"

They both spun to look at her, Jonathan unable to conceal a jolt of surprise.

Jonathan spoke directly to her. "So you know…" He turned away from them. "I'm not sure you want to know. Either of you. It's probably best if you don't."

"Mr. King, I'm not claiming that what you did or didn't do is any of my business. But somehow, there's this terrible connection between you, your son, and my father. I'm here because I need to understand."

"We need to know, Dad." Jackson's voice shook.

Jonathan turned toward them and began pacing in the space between the center table and the large brown leather couch. "It would have ruined your life, Jackson. You would have probably gone to jail. And with that on your record, Columbia would have been forced to rescind their offer. There's no way a publisher would have touched your book, either. The entire trajectory of your life would have been altered, based on one foolish decision."

Jackson tracked his father's movements, while Camille's gaze did not shift from her boyfriend's face.

Jonathan thrummed his fingers on the back of the couch. "Uncle Mason told me he knew an officer who had connections with the courts. That they could make this whole thing disappear. For a price."

Jackson bolted up out of his seat. "Holy shit, Dad! Do you know how illegal that is?"

The first sign of emotion crossed Jonathan's face. "Of course I do! I put everything at risk to save you. You had no idea what was happening."

Camille tugged at Jackson's arm, urging him to sit back down. "My father threw the case?"

"Yes, Camille. He and several others."

Jackson took two steps toward his father. "How much did you pay them?"

"Jackson, that's not important. It was a long time ago."

"How much did you pay them?" Jackson spoke more deliberately.

His father pressed his palm into the top of his forehead. "I don't know why that's rel-"

"I swear to God, Dad. I'm not going to ask nicely again." Jackson's face flushed with rage.

"Two million. About two million."

Camille squeezed Jackson's hand to stop the shaking in her body. "What about the woman? The one Jackson hit?"

"She's fine. Just fine. She's had a good life."

Two more steps closer. Camille watched as Jackson really began to lose his shit, the shape of his face and body transformed by rage. For an instant she wondered if Jackson was going to hit his father. "How could you possibly know that?"

"Jackson, you need to calm down. I know that she's fine because I've been taking care of her since the accident."

"Oh my God!" Jackson's bellow filled the large room.

Camille spoke over the mad pounding in her chest. "Taking care of her how?"

"I paid all her hospital bills. I got her a job. I help her with money, although she doesn't ask very much. I've been paying for her daughter's schooling."

"Do you have a relationship with her, Dad? Does she know what you did?"

"Do I look stupid to you?!" It was rare to see Mr. King so visibly perturbed. "She knows who I am. I told her that I felt bad about the verdict and offered to help her. We've kept in touch over the years. That's all."

"I've always struggled with the fact that I didn't understand you, Dad. But this... this proves that I had no idea who my father really was. Or is. I am horrified by what you did."

"Yes, Jackson," Mr. King seethed, "you get to be horrified. And sanctimonious. And judgmental. You know why? Because you didn't have to go to jail. And you didn't have a felony on your record. So before you start thinking how wrong I was, just imagine that life. The one you were supposed to have because of your carelessness and irresponsibility. The one I saved you from. You think this woman, who means the world to you, would have looked at you twice? Think about *that*."

Jonathan King stormed out of the room while Camille envisioned her own version of the ugly picture he painted. She imagined Jackson was doing the same.

Jackson tried to relax in the backseat of the car, grateful for the young man driving them home. He wasn't certain about Camille's state of mind, but his was completely unfit after what had happened with his father.

He got into bed and waited for her. She came in and sat on the edge of the bed with her back to him. He sat up.

"All my life, I've been lied to by the men around me. First my father, then yours, then you. I wish I understood what it was about me that would attract this into my life."

Jackson watched her shoulders move up and down with her short breaths. He wanted to show her the million ways that she was wrong. That he shouldn't be lumped in with those others, whose lies had, in fact, been detrimental to her life.

"Don't take this on, Cam. The ill deeds of others isn't yours to carry."

"I don't believe that. Not anymore. Sure, there was nothing I could've done about my father. I was a child and had no idea. But your father... I trusted him. He knew who I was, all these years, welcoming me into the family, knowing the terrible thing he'd done with my father." She turned slightly toward him.

"You know, it's not that different than what you did. All these years, lying to me about how you felt. I probably should've known. But I was so busy hiding my own secrets, I didn't try to see. Actually I tried *not* to see, because it was the scariest thing I've ever faced."

Jackson shook his head, praying that something helpful could come out of his mouth. "I'm not sure how this inquiry will benefit you."

"It's not about benefit to me. It's about realizing how every important man in my life was enveloped by secrets. Some of which hurt me. A lot."

"I'm sorry. For whatever part of that is mine. Actually I'm sorry for all of it. I wish you hadn't gone through any of it."

He crawled to her and pulled her into his arms. She pulled away.

"Does knowing what happened... what I did... does that change your perception of me?"

He wasn't ready for her to turn around so quickly to look him in the eye. He jerked back.

"There was probably a time I thought you were perfect. Those days are long gone, Jackson."

The muscles of his chest and abdomen contracted as if he'd been punched. "Wow."

She tilted her head and looked at him with an odd expression. It almost looked like confusion to him. "It's not a bad thing, necessarily. You shouldn't take it that way. I know who you are."

Jackson willed himself to slow down his breathing, to regain control, to not let the upset discolor this calm, but gut-wrenching, conversation. "I don't want you to think badly of me. I know the whole situation was wrong, but-"

"Please stop making it about you." Her voice had gone emotionless.

He nodded. "Fair enough. I just want you to know that-"

"I'm not going to dig into those cases anymore."

She spoke as if she'd been talking about the phone bill or what to have for dinner. He was so shocked by her delivery, he hardly registered her words.

She shrugged. "It's impossible to know who was right and who was wrong. Especially since the most important people in my life constantly obliterate that line. Isn't there some famous saying about sins of the father?"

She stood up as he reached for her. "I'm going to go read in the living room for a while. You stay here and sleep."

Several things became very clear to Jackson:

That was not a request.

The Grand Canyon sized rift in his beloved's heart would require a meticulous approach.

He'd thought nothing would be worse than the look of disgust she'd given him that evening. He was wrong. This was worse.

CHAPTER 15

*C*amille was determined to move forward, despite how terrible she felt. She and Jackson busied themselves with work and the mountain of details to complete the remodel of their new place. If she tried hard enough, she could make herself feel happy. After all, her life was nearly perfect. She was kicking ass in the career she loved, she had the man of her dreams, she was surrounded by people who loved her. Hell, even her house was going to be a showpiece. If only she could stop feeling like everything was tainted by secrets, betrayal, and disgrace.

"I think we should go away. Like we talked about before… everything."

She knew he was only trying to help. To distract her from the impenetrable darkness she couldn't shake. "It's not a good time, Jackson. We need to be accessible to the contractors and designers, and we're both busy with work."

He stopped her from rummaging through a box full of books and took her hands. "None of that matters right now, love. We'll delay the move. Or we'll take our chances that they'll get it right. It doesn't matter."

"But it does." It needed to matter. Or else she'd be stuck with all the other thoughts she didn't want to have.

"No, Camille. It doesn't. You're hurting. You're grieving. You're shocked. You're-"

She looked directly at him. "I'm not going anywhere, Jackson. I'm not going to run away from this. I'm not going to be afraid. I'm going to keep going, like I've always done. You might have noticed that I'm pretty good at it by now."

"Yes, I'm well aware of your competence." He dropped her hands. "I love you. I'm here for you. Whatever you need."

And then she encountered an expression she had never seen on that perfect face. Defeat.

CAMILLE ARRIVED HOME FROM WORK, after three days of awkward silence in her small house, looking forward to having some time on her own. She had urged Jackson to attend one of his numerous social events with his sister instead of her. She opened the door, already imagining the solitary delight of tucking herself into bed and not having to talk about a damn thing.

Her small ivory couch held two large dark-haired men with the same face. Jackson and Jonathan King stood up at the same time. She gripped the door handle, all of a sudden overtaken by exhaustion.

She turned toward them after closing the door. "Gentlemen."

"Camille. I hope you don't mind my surprise visit. I don't want to be presumptuous."

"It's alright, Dad."

Camille looked at Jackson and wondered why she hadn't been given a chance to answer. "I'm glad you're here, Mr. King. I have something for you."

She returned from the bedroom and handed the slip of

paper to the perplexed man. It took a single glance for him to recognize his own writing. "I don't understand."

"We're never going to cash that check. We accepted it just to be polite. You might as well take it back." *You're not going to be able to buy my forgiveness.*

Jonathan turned to his son.

Camille crossed her arms.

Jonathan broke the standoff. "I see you're still upset. Perhaps that's understandable. You've been through quite a lot recently."

"Please don't presume to understand what I've been through."

"Yes, yes, I suppose I couldn't. But I'd like to share something with you. About what I've been through."

The older man sat down, but both Camille and Jackson remained standing.

"I had two secrets that I thought I would take with me to the grave. And they've both been revealed. To you. I find that interesting. It seems to me that you think there are secrets all around you, but what I see is the opposite. Secrets falling apart around you."

That statement added just enough extra heaviness to her leaden body to bring her down onto the nearest seat.

"I know that one day, Camille, you will experience the feeling of protecting your child and maybe your beloved. What I did for Jackson, going against everything I stood for, I would do it again, many times over."

Jackson put his hand on his father's shoulder.

"And I can honestly say I would do it for you as well." He cleared his throat. "I care about you as much as any member of my family. Maybe even moreso. But I suppose that might not be something I should say aloud. Yes, I knew who you were from nearly the moment I met you. I'd been following your family since the trial. It terrified me at first, but then it came to me. This was a gift. This was a chance for me to redeem an act that contributed to another man's downfall."

Camille and Jackson looked at him curiously.

"I feel terrible for what happened to your father. To your parents. I feel like my desperate act contributed to the position he surely found himself in. But then you came into our family, and you were the most wonderful person I could imagine. I wanted everything for you. Everything that maybe you hadn't gotten from your own family. I kept that intention from you. That's true."

His gaze never left her face. She looked away.

"Those are my big secrets, Camille. But we all have them. Layers and layers of them. Even when we think we're being forthright and honest."

No, no, no, no, no.

He continued. "Maybe I've got a few more secrets too. Julian is gay. You are all tiptoeing around it, thinking I can't handle it. But I've known for some time. And I see how that secret is strangling his life. I know I'm old, but I'm not stupid. I mean, I'm pretty sure Bill Stevenson - you know my golf buddy? - I think he's gay. And-"

Jackson's arm wrapped around his father's broad shoulders. "Dad. I think we're veering off topic here." Both men laughed.

Camille couldn't bring herself to acknowledge what she'd seen and heard. Father and son were now the best of buddies. On the same side. If she could have plugged her ears to not hear them, she would have. All she wanted was to bury herself under the covers and hide from all this craziness. She was so very tired.

"That's what I came to say, my dear Camille. I hope that it has been helpful to you." He stood up. "Perhaps you see me differently, now. And maybe you don't like what you see. But it's still me. The man who treasures you with all his heart."

She looked up after the click of the door alerted her of his departure. Jackson leaned against the doorjamb. "Will you say something?"

"Your father knows about Julian. That's pretty funny."

"Dammit, Camille! Can you please address what just happened?"

"When did you two kiss and make up?"

His gaze dropped. "We've been talking. This mess has allowed us to really be honest with each other. It feels like a miracle."

She glowered at him. "Oh, how nice for you."

He took two long steps toward her. "Are you angry with me for bringing him here?"

"No."

"Are you angry with me for something else?"

"Nope."

"Will you talk to me about what you're feeling?"

She considered it. There was too much to say and not enough energy to do it. "No."

He dropped his head into his palm. Anger charred his breath. All the signs she'd come to recognize over the years appeared as he attempted to manage his exasperation.

He looked up. "Do you feel wronged by me or my father for what we did? Or for not having told you sooner?"

She sighed. "No. It had nothing to do with me. I mean, not directly."

"Oh, for fuck's sake, Cam. I can't do this. You're keeping me at arm's length. I have no idea what more to do."

"Don't do anything. There's nothing to be done." Camille knew her words sounded distant. Apathetic, even. She just couldn't muster the will to make it sound right.

He tilted his head back and groaned to the ceiling. "There's nothing you don't know about me. And if there is, it's because I've forgotten or I don't know about it either. Please don't shut me out. I'm dying here, Cam."

"You're dying? From what?" Bitterness tainted her words,

but it wasn't her intention. She was genuinely curious why he was feeling so hurt.

He walked into the kitchen, opened the highest cabinet above the stove, the one she couldn't reach, buried his arm in and pulled out a small, dark box.

Shock preceded recognition by several seconds. Not knowing where the energy came from, she was propelled onto her feet. He held out his outstretched arm, with the black velvet box balanced in the center of his palm. "Here's my most recent secret. I've been keeping it for almost two months."

Her head shook from side to side. A million questions enveloped her. None found their way through, but one. "Why?"

"It's the most important question I might ask, in my whole life. I don't want to be unsure about the answer." He closed his fingers around the tiny box and dropped his arm to his side. "I'm unsure about the answer."

"I can't do this now, Jackson. I'm sorry." She turned toward the bedroom, stepping out of her shoes on the way, pulled the bedding away and slid underneath. The resonant thud of the front door closing, much louder this time, penetrated even the numerous, heavy blankets.

There was no point in holding back or muffling her sobs. The house was empty, just as she had wished.

NOT A SINGLE ONE of Camille's tears was devoted to Jonathan King, who'd been an exemplary influence in her life and whom she'd treated unfairly. Not a single tear was for Jackson King, the love of her life. She'd pushed him away for no other reason than his love made it impossible to keep the pain away. Every single one of her tears were for the one man whose explanation or apology she would never receive: her father.

Not even coffee and aspirin dulled the headache she woke

up with. More sleep might have helped, but she was a woman on a mission.

The sun had not completely risen when she got into the car, took a few more sips of coffee, and began the long drive down to the St. Maria Goretti Cemetery.

Her visits had become less and less frequent over the past several years. She could make excuses about being too busy but it wasn't true. The wound of her parents' death had just refused to heal. Staying away felt like the only option for moving on.

She found her way instinctively to the large marble statue of the angel hovering over the two headstones. The ground had become overgrown. It had a general look of neglect. Camille got on her knees and wrapped her hand around a clump of dandelions. She pulled and cleared until there was enough open space to deposit the flowers she'd brought.

With dirt covering her hands, and body, she placed one palm on each patch of earth to either side of her and cried. The tears fell more softly than they had the previous night and a sense of emptiness began to replace the deep ache. She laid herself down, between them, and welcomed in the warmth of the brightening sun. To no one in particular, and everyone all at once, she whispered, "I forgive you."

She forced herself to remember good things. The day her father gave a talk at her school on career day, beaming at her the whole time. The trip she took with her mother to buy her first set of high heels, when they ate ice cream and shared silly jokes. Her poor mother, who might well have been an innocent victim. There was nothing to be done about it, regardless. Grief about her mother brought another wave of tears.

A chill woke Camille. She was surprised to have fallen asleep on the ground. Resolution strengthened her as she made the long walk back to the car. She took the final sip of her cooled coffee and plugged the next address into her navigation app.

She wiped some of the dirt off her jeans before walking into the police station, chuckling at the thought they might mistake her for a vagrant in her current state.

"I'm here to see Sergeant Williams, please," she told the woman in the glass fronted booth.

"Name and reason."

"I... uh... he's working on a case involving my parents. My name is Camille Moreau. Is he here?"

Without a greeting or response, the woman dialed the old-fashioned phone. "Camille Moreau here to see Williams."

Camille picked at her thumb as she watched the conversation.

"Go through the first waiting area and have a seat by the blue chairs. He'll be down in a minute."

BY THE TIME Camille returned to her car, the world around her already looked different. It was turning into one of those famously perfect fall days in San Francisco. She sat behind the wheel, relishing the feeling of the sun beaming through the windows. Her next destination wasn't as clear as the first two that morning. It could be one of a few places.

She pulled out of the parking lot and headed across town, debating until the very last minute where specifically she needed to go. She pulled up to the beautiful building and turned into the semi-circular entrance. A young valet, who looked like he hadn't quite recovered from his previous night out, greeted her. But who was she to judge, considering she was still mostly covered in dirt.

She walked across the lobby, smaller than she remembered from the few times they'd been there for Jackson's last book launch. The private club was well known by the city's poshest influencers. The apartment suites were legendary.

A woman, whose perfection gave her a slightly inhuman appearance, greeted her with a blinding smile. Camille grinned all the way to the private elevators, applauding herself for the masterful use of persuasion she'd learned from Jackson.

He did not immediately answer after her soft knock on the door. She raised her knuckles to try again when he appeared in the wide opening. "Camille…"

She stepped around him and into the room. "Hi."

"What are you doing here? How did you find me? How did you get past security?"

She laughed. "Oh, you think you're the only one who knows how to get what they want?"

"I can't believe…"

"I went to the cemetery."

His eyes sprung open. "You did?"

"Yeah. I spent the morning there. The plots were overrun with weeds. It was a mess. I'll have to call management about that." She looked at his face, but couldn't read his expression. "I was so mad at him, Jackson. Like, if he was still alive, I'd have wanted to kill him. Isn't that terrible? To be furious at someone who's already paid the ultimate price for his sins?"

"Cam…"

"So, we had a talk. I told him how I felt about what he did. And I told him that since I couldn't be mad at someone unable to defend themselves, I took it out on you. And your dad."

She thought she would have run out of tears by then, but she was wrong. "I'm sorry, Jackson. I'm sorry for what I did last night, when you…"

He reached out and took her hand.

"I'm sorry I wouldn't talk to you. It was just too hard. I wanted your apologies to be his apologies."

He pulled her into him. "I know, love. I know."

She exhaled into his arms and stayed there until their breathing synchronized. In. Out. Softening with each rise and fall.

He breathed into her hair. "I want you to know that I didn't leave out of anger. I was frustrated. It didn't feel like my presence was helping you. Maybe being on top of each other in the small space was making things worse for you. I didn't come here because I didn't want to be around you. I came here because... I'm willing to try anything to make you happy."

She looked up at him, then brought her lips to his. For the briefest moment, everything in the entire universe was perfect. "I know."

Before he dipped down for another kiss, she spoke. "There's more."

Those dark eyes opened wide. "More?"

"I went to see sergeant Williams. At the police station."

He mouthed the word 'wow' but no sound came out of his mouth. She might have actually stunned Jackson King. "We had a talk about the case and my parents and..."

Jackson looked at her, but didn't speak.

"I needed to know if they found what they needed. And if I was in any danger."

He took hold of her shoulders. "That was really brave of you, Cam. I know you swore you'd never go down there again."

"That was foolish. Like it or not, I'm involved. I can't just bury my head and pretend it's not happening."

He pulled her into him again, so tightly she thought she might break. "Love..."

She spoke into his chest. "He said it's done. All the dirty dominoes just fell."

His chuckle vibrated both of their bodies. "Dirty dominoes?"

She took one step back and looked at him, a smile plastered on that remarkable face. "That's cop-speak for bad guys, by the way."

"Does that mean...?"

"It's over. At least my part in it. I'm not sure it'll ever be the same as before I knew everything, but it's as good as I imagined it could be. I'm... okay."

"You amaze me. Constantly." Jackson gave her that look, the one she'd seen many times, but always took her by surprise.

It was always too much to be in the beam of his focus. For the first time since entering the room, Camille glanced around. "This place... I think it's bigger than my whole house."

He nodded. "Maybe..."

"I think we should stay here. I've loved having you so close all the time, but I think the chaos of all our stuff is making me batty. I need-"

"Anything, love. I think they have an even bigger model, if you want more room. We can stay here as long as you like."

"I don't need more room. I need you. And daily maid service."

He cupped her cheek, his breath catching. "God, I missed you, Cam."

"I'm back." A brown smudge on her palm caught her eye. "And I think a shower might be on top of the list of what I need."

CHAPTER 16

*C*amille emerged from the shower, wrapped from head to toe in the bright white plush robe and towels emblazoned with the gold crest of the hotel. He hadn't even noticed that she was covered in dirt, until after she pointed it out. Seeing her at his door felt like the sun rising. Nothing could be wrong in a world where Camille loved him. She was his everything.

"I ordered some food."

"Perfect."

"But first…" He patted the sheet on the recently turned down bed. Her soft smile filled the room with light. She'd shed everything covering her body by the time she crawled into the bed and disappeared under the bedding. He walked around to the other side, stripped down, and slid in beside her, finding her grinning like a girl on Christmas morning.

Her eyes raked over his body, which was demonstrating its readiness for her.

"Pretty nice in here, right?" Jackson said.

Her palm slid from his chest, down his abdomen, and around to his bottom. "I want to spend a lot of time in this bed."

"I think I can manage that."

He pressed her body into his, their mouths meeting in a burst of wet heat. He wanted to be gentle, to take his time, to savor their reconnection, but the immense desire he felt for her exceeded his ability to manage it. He threw the covers off his overheated body and rolled her onto her back, hands stroking and squeezing anything he could hold.

The rose of her flushed cheeks caught his eye and he stopped, hovered over her. "God, Cam... I'm going too fast. Sorry. It's just-"

"Don't stop. Don't slow down."

Like a burst of wind on an already blazing fire, her words created an inferno in his body. His hand slipped between her legs and dipped inside her. His mouth watered at the wetness coating his fingers and her delightful moan of pleasure. He created a trail of kisses from her mouth to where his fingers had been pressing into her and stroking. Her fingers dragged across his scalp as he pulled her clit between his lips. Nothing in his life felt like having his face between her legs.

Her body was the gift that kept giving. Every time he thought he'd found her rhythm, her pattern, another melody was revealed. She bucked her hips, pushed and pulled at his head and shoulders, and called out his name with each round of orgasm. He could have spent the rest of the day enjoying her exquisite body.

He lifted his head to see her, mouth open, hand cradling her breast, deep, resonant groans vibrating her entire body. She looked down, eyes sparkling and electric. A mischievous grin was followed by a squeeze of her thighs. Before he understood what was happening, she rolled their bodies and mounted him, palms pressing into his chest. Her eyes blazed into him with an intensity that kept him from moving or questioning or breathing. The sensation of entering her - hot, tight, wet - nearly broke his own focus. A burst of desperate need sent a tremor through his body. Decades of mastery exploded into a singular thought: Give her everything.

Her small hands tightened around his wrists and dragged them above his head. She couldn't have actually pinned him but that look of feral power transmitted a message that all the cells of his body understood. She stroked the length of him with her whole body, joy coloring her cheeks, breasts bouncing, hair flying. He longed to feel her in his hands and on his mouth, but he let himself be hers to use as she wished. Her panting became groaning and hands moved from his wrists to the nape of his neck. She lifted his head to meet her mouth, and cried out her orgasm into him. Her pulses vaulted him into his own as his hands found her ass and ground her into him.

Minutes passed before she dropped the weight of her body onto him. The moisture of her skin began to cool and he wrapped his arms more tightly around her. A slight roll to one side brought her back onto the bed, a position where he could see her better. With each breath, she softened more and more, the wild ferocity replaced by a fullness and calm he hadn't seen on her face in too long.

Jackson willed himself to stay present, stay awake, to watch her as she relinquished her hold and let herself be taken into rest. He'd spent a lifetime mastering the power play between people, understanding the subtle pulls and shifts that communicate command. He'd also known the immense well of power that lay beneath the quiet competence of the woman he loved. When she took control of both their bodies, it wasn't the first time he'd seen her fully tap into it, but it was the first time he understood what it meant to her.

This was Camille's declaration. She'd fought her whole life to not be the victim, even when the world around her conspired to make it so. Her powerlessness around the deeds of her father had shaken the entire foundation of her life. Instead of crumbling, she grew stronger.

He stayed focused while she slept, his mind formulating and creating, his body still so as not to disturb her. He stared at her beautiful face and wondered how he'd gotten it so wrong. All his assertions and presumptions about who she was and what their relationship would be couldn't have been further from reality. He didn't know if he'd missed the signs, all these years, or if she'd never shown him. She defied everything he thought he knew. Camille Moreau was nothing short of magical.

By the time she fluttered her eyes open, his mind had connected so many threads in his own life, he was buzzing with excitement.

She squinted at him, sleep still in her eyes. "Hey, lover."

He kissed her on the tip of her nose. "Hi, love. How was your nap?"

"So very, very good."

He brushed the hair from her cheek. "I think you needed that."

"Yup."

"I wanted to talk to you about some things."

She blinked several times. Worry created a small crease between her brows.

"All good. I promise. So, I know you don't want to go back into those cases anymore. I don't blame you. But I think there's another way to approach restitution. Let's create a foundation. Put all the money in it. Get even more from donations. And we can donate to legal defense funds for at-risk populations. Or kids. Or whatever."

Her face remained emotionless. His mind snapped to all that might have been wrong with his suggestion. "What do you think?"

"I love it, Jackson. That's brilliant. But I don't know anything about foundations or nonprofits or that whole world."

"That's okay. We know two people who do. Ramona and my mother."

She wrapped her arms around him and kissed his neck.

"I have more."

She pulled away. "More?"

"I've been thinking about your job. I want to take back my

suggestion to stay at Google. I think if getting in on an early stage venture sounds exciting to you, you should do it. You deserve to be the driving force behind something great, the star, not just another cog in someone else's empire."

"That's nice of you to say, honey. I've been thinking about it too." She took a heavy breath. "It might not be appropriate at this point. I won't have my financial safety net anymore. I might have to-"

"Camille, I would really like you to stop thinking that you're on your own. I know it's been that way for most of your life, but it's not that way now. I couldn't be more willing to be your safety net. Hell, if you wanted to quit altogether and lay on the couch all day, that would be fine with me."

Her expression clearly indicated she didn't like any part of his suggestion.

"I know you didn't want to talk about it when we were making plans for the house. But it needs to be clear. I take financial responsibility for us. Completely. If you want to keep your fat-cat salary and whisk me away on sexy getaways, I'm fully down for that. If you want to volunteer teaching girls to code, that's wonderful. I really mean it when I say I want you to consider our financial future taken care of."

"I don't understand. Why is this such a hard line for you?"

He looked toward the abstract painting on the wall before turning back to her. "It's just something I decided. Long time ago."

This jerked her up to sitting. "No way. You don't do anything without a full analysis. What aren't you telling me?"

He didn't like the squint of her eyes. She was looking right through him. "Why can't I just want to-"

"Spill it, Jackson."

"It's what my father did!" Even though his tone was much harsher than he wanted, she didn't flinch. A small nod greeted him, instead.

"Tell me more, love. What did your father do?"

This wasn't a story he could tell laying down. He propped himself up and took a breath. "My dad was just this poor kid from Newark, New Jersey. My mom's family owns most of Virginia. Really old money and lots of it. He had to fight against so much to be with her, including claims that he'd never be able to support her. But he decided he would. And he never took a penny of her family's money. He did it all on his own."

"How do you know this?"

"My aunt Olivia, my mother's sister-"

"The one married to the Congressman?"

"Yeah. She's never been a great fan of my father's, but she told me this story as a lesson in integrity. I could see the respect in her eyes." He caught her gaze. "That's what I want. That's the kind of man I want to be."

Camille bit her trembling lip.

He knew exactly what was going on in that brilliant mind of hers: How come he'd never told her this story? "I know what you're thinking."

Everything about her expression softened. "I'm thinking that the person underneath the official Jackson King is a man I find to be remarkable in every way."

He couldn't suppress a surprised smile. "Oh."

She wove her fingers through his. "I want to say something… about yesterday."

So much had happened in the previous twenty four hours. Most of it wasn't particularly good. He braced himself. "Yes."

"What happened, after your father left, I'm really sorry. I was so rude at a moment you were being vulnerable and it was terrible of me."

Relief coursed through his veins, releasing the knot at the base of his throat. "Actually, I was wrong. It was intense emotional manipulation on my part in a desperate attempt to get a reaction from you. You were struggling and it wasn't fair or kind of me. I wish I could take it back. That's certainly not how I want our proposal to go."

Her eyebrows shot up, which made him smile. "I'm sure you weren't surprised that that's where we're headed, right?"

Her cheeks flushed. "Well, yes and no. I was surprised at that moment."

He nodded. "Understandable. So, even though I'm the one who screwed up, I'm hoping you'll give me another chance. To do it right. The way you deserve."

She pulled his face to her and kissed him until they were both out of breath.

~

Six months earlier

"Do you think he'll propose?" Jenna stood in front of the wall of mirrors pulling at the bust-line of her newly altered bridesmaid dress.

"No way. I think Charlie's more likely to break up with me. I told you - he's been acting so strange lately. Jealous and angry, but he won't come out and say it." Camille frowned at her own garish, ill-fitting dress.

"Guys are like that. They act all weird when they're nervous about something. And why would he fly all the way across the country with you just to break up? That doesn't make any sense."

"I guess." Camille looked at her beautiful best friend, who couldn't even make a terrible bridesmaid dress look bad. "That looks great on you, by the way."

"It's terrible. And doesn't fit around the top at all. I'm afraid with one dance move, I'm going to fall right out."

"I think mine is too tight around my hips. See how it does that weird thing?" Camille ran her hand across the puckered fabric on her lower belly.

"Anyway, back to the important stuff. If he asks, what will you say?"

Camille waited as a saleswoman escorted a bride-to-be to

the adjacent fitting area. "I can't marry Charlie. I love him, the past two years have been fine, but he's not *the one*. I thought you hated him anyway?"

"Yeah, he's not my favorite. But if he makes you happy, that's what matters."

"I'm not sure that's true anymore." Camille huffed out a sigh. Breakups sucked. She didn't want that either. "Let's get through this trip to Chicago and the wedding. We can reassess when we get back home." Maybe this trip would reignite their spark. It had been good… once.

"Maybe Charlie will bow out before we go, then you'll be free to scope out all the hot single guys at the wedding. You must remember some of Doug's friends."

"Yes, the groom has some attractive friends. But I'm not even out of this relationship. I don't need to be thinking about the next one." Besides, breaking up with Charlie would confirm he had a right to be angry with her.

"It's because of my brother, isn't it?"

Camille's head whipped around. "What's that supposed to mean?"

"With him satisfying every one of your needs, who needs a boyfriend?"

"You and I both know that he is not satisfying *every* one of my needs."

"I am completely certain he would. All you have to do is ask."

"Jenna, I would more likely sleep with you than sleep with Jackson."

Jenna puckered and shrugged. "I'd consider it, Cammy. You're super hot, a great kisser, and with enough tequila…"

Camille threw her arms up. "You are impossible!"

Jenna lunged forward for a hug, dropping both women to the ground in a puddle of laughter and crimson taffeta.

～

Now

Camille closed her eyes and warmed her face in the late afternoon sun. It was a rare, crystal clear day, and the deck of their newly remodeled home might have been the most perfect spot in the whole city of San Francisco.

When Jackson joined her, bearing two glasses of champagne, she wondered how this was now her life. "I can't believe you found the glasses, honey."

"Aaaah, I packed them in my bag. I didn't want to chance not finding them in the disarray."

Behind them was a house full of boxes, which they would get to, eventually. But their first day back, they chose to make all celebration and no work.

While Camille melted into the remarkable view, Jackson filled the glasses. "Tell me what you're thinking, love," he asked.

"I'm in awe. The house is even more beautiful than I imagined. All the effort has been well worth it."

"I'm so glad you feel that way. I have to say I was worried it wouldn't compare with the Four Seasons."

"We brought all the good things from the Four Seasons with us."

"Like our everlasting love? Like our renewed commitment? Like-"

"Like our new cleaning lady, who has indefinite 'favorite person' status from me."

"Wow. How easily I'm replaced."

"Only for one thing, darling. You are even more terrible than me at keeping house."

"Which says something."

She slapped his arm and gave him a pretend scowl.

"Stealing Saskia away from the hotel was merely one of your numerous, consistently brilliant ideas."

"I think having an orderly space will go a long way in maintaining my mental health."

"Whatever you want is yours, my love."

She beamed at him, still incredulous about all they'd been through. "These past five months have been crazy."

"To say the least. With the small renovation that ended up being a whole house remodel, the drama with my family, then your family…"

"Not to mention us living on top of each other in my cottage."

"There are much, much worse things than living on top of you, my darling."

She grinned at her sexy man. "We did pretty well, didn't we?"

"I'm sure each of my siblings were taking bets about how long it would take for you to throw me out. But I loved every minute, Cam. I can't imagine having survived this summer with anybody else by my side."

"How do you like the house?"

"I loved the house before. But you've managed to create something I love even more. It's kind of like how I feel about you. I don't know how it's possible that in these months, facing nearly every stress a couple can face, I've grown to love you even more. What we had before was nothing, like puppy love."

Camille swallowed a lump in her throat. "I feel the same way. I'm excited to start our lives together, here in our amazing home. It's like a dream come true, really."

He reached out and took her hand, something serious darkening his expression. "Cam, I want your life to feel like a dream, for you to feel like you are the most loved woman on the planet." He paused to touch his lips to the top of her hand. "From the very beginning, you've given me everything I wanted. You said yes to being my friend, and then my best friend. You said yes to my family, needing to possess you. You said yes to being my lover," his voice cracked, "and then yes to creating a home with me." His face reddened. "There's one more thing I'm hoping you will say yes to."

Camille's heart knew what was happening well before her mind made sense of the movement of his hand into his pocket, and the retrieval of something out of it. She had almost forgotten about that day, in the depth of her darkness, when she'd first seen that small velvet box.

"Camille Annalise Moreau, will you marry me?"

There was no question. "Of course, Jackson. Yes. I will."

When he slipped the ring onto her finger, she held her breath. The large diamond caught a ray of light and sparkled, breaking through the clouded view of her tear-filled eyes. Her hand, shaky and heavy, settled onto his open palm.

She pulled her gaze from the polished platinum band and single emerald-cut stone - a simple, elegant design that exactly matched her vision of the perfect ring. His face beamed, molten chocolate eyes clouded by their own tears.

Camille had known, for a long time, that it would be forever with Jackson King. Well before rings, and houses, and romantic dates, and dance lessons. She'd known from the moment he looked at her across the table, those eyes speaking directly to her heart, that he was the one.

And that secret, she'd kept for a very long time.

<<<THE END>>>

Dearest Reader,

I HOPE you enjoyed Camille and Jackson's remarkable love story. If you'd like to share your thoughts about the book with others, I'd be delighted for your review at your preferred book retailer. Reviews support independent authors!

For all the perks of being a cherished reader (which you are), and be the first to know about new releases, sign up to be part of the Smart & Sexy Reader Team. I regularly send out book bonuses, audio clips, playlists and other goodies to make the wild ride even more fun. Get on the list at http://bit.ly/PEKSignup.

If you can't wait to find out what happens next, flip the page to find an excerpt of Coming Home, the next book in the Friends & Lovers Series.

Thank you again, and I hope to see you soon between the pages of my steamy love stories.

Excerpt from COMING HOME
Book Two of the Friends & Lovers Series

A bit of melted Cheddar oozed out between crisp slices of bread, warming the corner of Ramona's mouth. She flicked out her tongue and caught the errant piece of deliciousness. The sharp tang, tempered by something earthy and creamy, pushed a satisfied groan up from the bottom of her belly. This was turning out to be a whole body eating experience.

With one more bite, the first piece was gone. She looked up from the other half of the sandwich, cut into a perfect triangle, crusts removed, to find Lucas' gaze intent on her. "I have to say, your grilled cheese sandwiches are even better than I remember. Even though they were always amazing."

Lucas leaned forward, tanned forearms on the expanse of the stainless steel worktable. "Glad to see my extensive culinary education wasn't a complete waste of time."

She picked up the remaining piece and paused, deciding to exercise the tiniest bit of self-control and not put the whole thing in her mouth. "No. I think you picked right. All this scrumptious food would have been wasted on a bunch of stuffy lawyers."

A shrug accompanied a dimple-enhanced grin. "Except those stuffy lawyers are now my main customers."

"Lucky them." She took one more bite and licked each of her fingers, giving up on manners. After all, this was Lucas, the boy who'd been by her side for the first half of her life. Absence of their hard-earned etiquette wasn't going to offend him. What he was feeding her was much too delicious to hold back.

He pulled a champagne bottle from the industrial-sized refrigerator and refilled her glass. "I still can't believe you're here, in my kitchen. After all this time."

"Gotta thank Connor for that. My brother's been nearly impossible to reach lately, but he made sure I knew how to find your restaurant. I don't do airplane food." Ramona wondered how much her brother had told his best friend, Lucas, about her over the years. Did he know how much time she spent on planes and her refusal to touch any of that food?

"How come you got in so late? He told me you'd be here by eight or nine."

"Oh, sorry." She gave him what she hoped expressed remorse. When your life depended on air travel, getting anywhere on time was always risky. Besides, she liked having the restaurant, and the chef, all to herself. "There was *weather* in San Francisco, as always. And we hit a bunch of traffic as we approached downtown D.C."

"Did you give your driver the shortcut?"

She shook her head. "How would I know a shortcut?"

He laughed. "Right. I keep forgetting how you never come home anymore."

This hasn't been home for a really long time. "Anyway, I really appreciate your staying open so late and cooking me all my favorites. I didn't mean to take advantage."

"Mowgli, I can't think of any way I'd rather spend this night than feeding you."

She flattened her palm on the cool steel worktable. His oh-too-sultry smirk generated even more heat in the warm kitchen. "Speaking of which, can you make me another grilled cheese?"

"But you haven't even finished this one. And I have a few more things for you to try tonight."

Ramona shifted on the cold stool. Why did everything he said sound like an innuendo? "It's for tomorrow. For breakfast."

"That's a terrible idea. It's going to be inedible tomorrow." He thrummed his fingers on the counter. "You can just come back and I'll make you a fresh one."

Her eyebrows cinched in confusion. "Uh, I'm going to be a bit busy tomorrow."

He frowned. "Right. I forgot. Sorry."

She emptied her glass in one gulp. "No worries." She wished she could forget, too.

Lucas pulled a towel from a hook and turned around to wipe along the edge of the cooktop. His broad shoulders shimmied as he worked a particular spot, sandy brown curls grazing the top of his white chef's jacket.

Ramona sucked in a breath, trying not to ogle the remarkable sight. He definitely didn't look like he'd been partaking of his rich, restaurant food. All the chubby softness of his youth had transformed into a rock solid wall of a man.

He turned just as her gaze hovered around his bottom. Her eyes didn't move nearly fast enough to play it off. It was impossible to know if he knew that she was staring. And what she was staring at.

He shook the towel out. "What's up, Mo?"

Something in the sweetness of his voice switched on a memory of a life she had all but tucked away. "It feels like no time has passed. Like we're kids again."

His smile broadened. "Except that instead of being noon, it's midnight."

"And we're in your phenomenal restaurant, instead of my mom's kitchen."

He looked down and swiped a crumb from the counter. "And I've learned how to clean up after myself."

"Looks like you've learned a lot of things. Including how to grow facial hair." *And a super hot bod.*

He stroked his close cropped goatee. "Yeah, I've had that one down for some time now. Speaking of growing things, I see all those prayers for boobs finally paid off."

Ramona's mouth opened with a dramatic gasp, heat blazing her cheeks, and a laugh threatening to dissolve her efforts at propriety. "That is completely inappropriate."

"Oh, come on, Mo. I was the first one to ever touch them, if you remember."

It wasn't possible to keep a straight face. "There was nothing there to touch."

"Oh, there was plenty. Trust me." He tilted his head and looked up toward the open pipework of the ceiling. "It was the highlight of my boyhood. Maybe of my entire life."

So hard not to check out her own chest, make sure everything was full and lofty. "I would have hoped you'd made some more substantial memories than my non-existent teenage boobs."

"I appreciate your confidence in me, but you seriously underestimate how great they were." He cupped his hands, and sighed. "Small, but perfect."

She shook her head and chuckled, keeping her eyes straight ahead. *Don't look down, Ramona.*

"By the way… not small anymore." He wasn't trying to keep his eyes away.

"Okay, you seriously have to stop talking about my breasts." And staring at them. "You're acting like you're fifteen again." She stopped herself from crossing her arms in front of her chest, afraid it would bring even more attention to the area.

"I feel fifteen again, with you here."

Time to regain control of this conversation. "It's great to see you, Baloo. Really great." Too great, maybe. "And I would love if you could get on with making whatever else you intend to feed me. I'm still hungry."

The left side of his mouth quirked upward in the grin she would know anywhere, even though it was on a face she hadn't seen in a very long time. A face, complete with broad jaw, full lips and a hint of a wrinkle in the corner of his eyes. A manly man's face. "Glad to see the bossiness hasn't changed."

"Haven't quite outgrown that one, I suppose."

He turned on a burner and slid a shiny pan over the flame. "Good."

She scanned the entirety of the bright kitchen, anything to avoid staring at him while he prepared her next goodies.

Lusting after her childhood buddy during a quick trip to town was not a smart maneuver. Too many connections would make it impossible to cut-and-run. And when it came to spending time in Virginia, less was more.

He made an almost imperceptible growl in response to whatever was happening on the cooktop. His large hand wiped down the side of his chef pants, highlighting that bottom again. It was useless. She dropped her chin into her palm and just let herself enjoy the view.

Two plates slid toward her, piled with colors as vibrant as the cover of any cookbook. Tart tomato salad and bright green dumplings in a sesame broth brought her closer to satisfaction, but not completely. She looked up from the empty plates with a sheepish grin.

Without a pause, or even a hint of judgment in those hazel eyes, he cleared them away. "Okay, Mo, I've got one more thing."

She was pretty sure he had quite a bit more than *one more thing*. "Great. I need to use the loo, though."

"Use the one in my office." He pointed toward a bowl big enough for her to bathe in. "Just past the mixer and down the hall. I'll bring the final course to you."

"Perfect."

Ramona used the bathroom quickly, averting her eyes from all the mirrors. Thoughts she shouldn't be having made it hard to look at herself. She and Lucas... well, their childhood bond had cracked a long time ago. But the combination of tender nostalgia and sharp desire was making it much too easy to succumb to a very adult fantasy. Besides, Lucas was flirting back. She was sure of it.

She stepped back into the office, large and full, but not messy. No sign of Lucas, so she walked in a slow circle around the space. It was oddly shaped, with almost no parallel walls, several of which were glass, offering a panoramic view of the kitchen. A wide bookcase held ancient-looking cookbooks, and an entire wall, behind a modern white lacquer desk, was graced with framed diplomas, certificates, and letters. She pushed the desk chair aside to examine his awards.

It was impressive. Accolades from two different culinary schools and various specialty programs around the world. Articles about his first restaurant, and now this newer one. Awards for being named a top young chef three years in a row, and pictures with two presidents. He walked in as she examined the row of five framed letters clearly different than all the rest. They were handwritten and adorned with pencil and crayon drawings, all addressed to Mr. Chef Lucas.

A clang of metal caught her attention. He'd set a large tray on the bench against the back wall, holding another bottle of champagne, as well as several plates with desserts that looked like pieces of art.

As she approached him, her eyes swept over the assortment and her mouth watered. "Wow, Baloo. Is that all for me?"

"For us." He poured a flute of champagne, which made her wonder what had happened to her previous glass. "Start with this."

Slightly bolder than the first bottle, with a hint of peach at the finish. "Spectacular."

"And now this." He put something the color of mocha into her mouth. It melted almost instantly into a sweet, spicy, brandy-tinged bolt of utter mouth happiness.

She walked back over to the desk. "That's a pretty impressive wall over there. Much more so than a silly law degree."

"Says the woman who actually finished law school. And passed the bar."

That seemed so long ago. "Not that I'm practicing law, either."

He swept the hair that had fallen across her forehead over to the side. "You know, I can see that you've been getting proper haircuts, Mo, but it still seems to fall over your eyes."

"Well, it's fashionable now."

He kept his palm on her cheek. "I still can't believe I'm looking at your face. More beautiful than ever."

His finger grazed her jawline and lifted her chin. The perfect start to a kiss, had they been different people.

Ramona turned around to face the award wall, mostly to compose herself and certain she could not hide how very much she wanted him to kiss her. Damn. Indecision sucked, but that's all she could muster.

She pointed to the hand-written letters. "Tell me about those."

He moved directly behind her, his body pressed into her back. She placed her palms on the desktop to steady the nearly imperceptible tremor that was developing in response to the pressure of his body on hers.

He exhaled next to her ear. "Oh, my kids." A sweet sigh followed. "They're from Chisholm Elementary, on the southside. I go over there a couple of times a year and do a cooking class, and we talk about healthy food. I love those kids. Sweetest, smartest, most alive people I know. Some of their lives are beyond disastrous. And yet, they are amazing."

He rested his chin on the top of her shoulder.

"Looks like they love you back, Mr. Chef Lucas."

A synchronized breath softened her back into his chest. He wrapped his arm around her waist. A lightening-fast analysis of pros and cons played itself in her head.

Pro: This was Lucas. She'd never been closer to another human being in her life.

Cons: 1). This was Lucas. They hardly knew each other anymore.

2). The cause of her return home to Virginia might deserve some propriety.

3). This wouldn't be a one-night stand she could run away from.

Pro: This was Lucas. The boy with a heart of gold who'd become a man who was hot as hell. Hotter than hell, probably.

Con: This was-

Fuck it.

In an unprecedented display of boldness, she took his hand and moved it from her hip to her belly, then slowly slid it up, over her ribs and finally grazing over her left breast, where she kept it.

When his fingers squeezed softly, a scratchy breath escaped him. She placed her palms back on the desk and used the leverage to press her bottom into him, eliminating any space between their bodies. From his chest to his legs, everything behind her was hard as steel.

His hand moved up to her throat, then down again, this time inside the deep opening of her dress. He cupped her breast while the other hand slid down her outer thigh, over her skirt, then back up underneath it. She stepped her legs further apart.

"Ramona…" His fingers slid beneath the front of her thong.

Warm finger, hot breath, all *yes*. It was increasingly hard to keep up as hands lifted her skirt and pulled her thong down, returning to graze her wetness.

She reached behind her to find the bulge beneath his zipper. Even through his pants, it was evident that there was something significant between his legs and it was rock hard. She clumsily tried to undo his belt buckle while swirling in the sensation of the finger that had just entered her.

He completed the task of removing his pants, evident by the metallic clink of his belt hitting the floor, and then the feel of his cock where his finger had been. He stopped.

"Fuck me, Lucas."

Hesitation gone, he pushed inside her in successive strokes. She willed herself to relax, to take him in, even as her entire body wanted to contract with the craving for him. They moaned in matching octaves. She thought she might burst with the fullness of him, and that would be a perfectly acceptable way to go.

He stopped. Again. "I need to see you."

He pulled out of her and spun her toward him, taking her

mouth in a fierce embrace and preventing her from catching a glimpse of his cock before it disappeared between her legs again. She perched her bottom on the edge of the desk and opened herself for him. He entered her in a graceful stroke. The wetness dripping from her and having coated him gave him ample lubrication to plunge into her.

She grabbed his neck and molded her mouth on his while he wrapped his arm around her, keeping her from falling back. With each stroke she groaned louder until that familiar build-up in the deepest part of her belly. The need for a breath pulled her away from his lips and brought her face down to the top of his shoulder, which she bit in matching intensity to the orgasm that cascaded over her.

He slowed as she did.

"Don't stop. Please."

"I'm going to-"

"Yes." Her hands moved to his buttocks and pressed him deeper. His hand slapped the wall when a growl escaped his throat. Each pulse of his orgasm sent a jolt up her spine and she held on for dear life.

"Holy shit." His body continued shaking as she took his face in her hands.

She ran her tongue along the thick edge of his lower lip and then stuck it in between. The ferocity of their desire gave way to something much more tender and intimate. They kissed like that, as they might have as teenagers, until the cold desk created a shiver up her spine.

She pulled away to catch her breath. He loosened the grasp around her waist and slid out of her.

"Ramona…"

There was nothing she could possibly say.

He stared into her eyes. "Are you okay?"

His semen ran down the inside of her leg. "Yes. Of course."

She wanted to get to the bathroom but each move sent

another trail of cum farther down, now into her shoes. He didn't let go.

She gave him one more kiss before moving him tenderly away.

He helped smooth her dress after he had put his underwear and pants back on. "I now have one less item on my bucket list."

She halted the search for her underwear. Had he really just said… "Fucking someone on your desk?"

"No." He fumbled with the buttons on his jacket. "Being with you."

He really did say it. "Having sex with me was on your bucket list?"

"Since I was eleven." His cheek quivered.

"Wow." Her teenage mind hadn't taken their explorations that far. And this was one hell of a strange postcoital conversation.

"That's not really how I imagined it, though." He grazed her arm. "A bit less fast and furious, maybe."

The room wasn't big enough to contain the enormity of her discomfort. "I need to go clean up. I'll be right back."

She stood in the bathroom for longer than was necessary. This time, there was no avoiding all those mirrors. Eyeliner had smeared across her cheek and her lips were puffy and red. Her hand shook as she threw cold water on her face. It didn't do anything to still her growing anxiety.

She had just fucked her childhood friend. The boy she thought she'd always love but hadn't seen in fifteen years. It was amazing, no doubt, but wrong. Probably wrong. Maybe not wrong?

Ugh. Either way, she was in no position to address either his confession or their transgression. She tried to wrangle her hair behind her ears, but it was a lost cause. Deep breath in, deep breath out. Maybe it wasn't as bad as she thought. Maybe this night would turn out to be a fun highlight of an otherwise dreadful visit. They could be cool, right? At least long enough for her to do what she needed to do, then get the hell out of town.

Lucas was looking down at his hands when Ramona stepped back into the office. She was not a stranger to sticky situations, but this was a whole different type of challenge. *God, this is awkward.* "It's getting late."

"Let me take you home, Mo."

Anything to not have to keep facing him, hair mussed by her own hand. And not from a rough game of touch football on his front lawn. "Sure, thanks."

They sat silently during the car ride across town. She hoped her father had kept the door unlocked, as she had requested. She didn't want anything delaying a speedy entry into the house.

Lucas took her hand after parking in her father's narrow driveway. "I know this is strange. But it doesn't have to be. It's still just me... Baloo."

"That's what makes it strange." She reached over and gave him a small kiss. "Good night, Lucas."

"See you tomorrow."

The deep smile on his remarkable face was nearly enough to hold down her rising dread about the day that would begin in only a few more hours. The entire reason for her trip.

"Yes. See you tomorrow."

∾

Find out what happens next.
COMING HOME is available wherever fine books are sold.

ALSO BY

PE KAVANAGH

FRIENDS & LOVERS SERIES

Collecting Secrets (Book One)

Coming Home (Book Two)

Claiming Power (Book Three)

Consenting Adults (Book Four)

ZODIAC MAGIC SERIES

Casting A Spell (Book One)

THE PRICE SERIES

The Price of Desire (Book One)

Sex, Money, and the Price of Truth (Book Two)

Available at your favorite online retailers.

GRATITUDES

As with most of the stories that consume me, this one held a firm grip. Jackson, Camille, their families and friends fought for my attention, resulting in the first three books of the Friends & Lovers Series. They are characters who've succeeded and failed in equal measure, and whose yearning to be seen and heard and loved stole my own heart.

There are always so many to thank...

The intrepid readers undaunted by the story in its clunky, messy beginnings and who helped me excavate the most gleaming story I could write. Special thanks to my beloved Scribophile groups.

My darling, the Latin hottie who tells me how wonderful all my writing is (even when it isn't) and is always hungry for more.

My girl, who isn't strictly allowed to read my books, but always has a remarkably helpful opinion to share about human behavior, fonts, and Photoshop.

And you. Of course, you, who chose to come along on the wild adventure with me. We've got so much more fun in store for us.

ABOUT THE AUTHOR

I believe that everything we experience exists as a story within us.

My journey as a writer includes the award-winning poem I penned at the ripe old age of seven, decades of hiding and doubt, and then finally... finally!... realizing that art needs to be shared. Storytelling is part of my heritage, even though I denied it for so long. The stories I created - true and imaginary - have saved me numerous times.

My characters come to me, like old friends excited to tell me what's new.
They represent the world I see and the world I want to see.

More than anything, I care about recovery from life's setbacks... getting back on your feet after life has brought you to your knees... and my characters fight the hard fight for the lives they know are waiting for them.

I've drawn my inspiration from the many flavors of my life experience. Once a sad, shy girl, I've also been an MIT-trained engineer, biotech executive, professional dancer, yoga teacher and business owner, school founder, spiritual counselor, entrepreneur, and author.

And I own a magic wand that I'm certain will work one day.

When I'm not typing furiously trying to capture the stories

that pour from me, you can find me loving my people to excess, globe-trotting to the next great adventure, and sporting bright red lips as a tango diva. And of course on my digital homes: pekavanagh.com and boldsoulcoaching.com.